Major Haynes of The Secret Service by Edgar Wallace

Richard Horatio Edgar Wallace was born on the 1st April 1875 in Greenwich, London. Leaving school at 12 because of truancy, by the age of fifteen he had experience; selling newspapers, as a worker in a rubber factory, as a shoe shop assistant, as a milk delivery boy and as a ship's cook.

By 1894 he was engaged but broke it off to join the Infantry being posted to South Africa. He also changed his name to Edgar Wallace which he took from Lew Wallace, the author of Ben-Hur.

In Cape Town in 1898 he met Rudyard Kipling and was inspired to begin writing. His first collection of ballads, The Mission that Failed! was enough of a success that in 1899 he paid his way out of the armed forces in order to turn to writing full time.

By 1904 he had completed his first thriller, The Four Just Men. Since nobody would publish it he resorted to setting up his own publishing company which he called Tallis Press.

In 1911 his Congolese stories were published in a collection called Sanders of the River, which became a bestseller. He also started his own racing papers, Bibury's and R. E. Walton's Weekly, eventually buying his own racehorses and losing thousands gambling. A life of exceptionally high income was also mirrored with exceptionally large spending and debts.

Wallace now began to take his career as a fiction writer more seriously, signing with Hodder and Stoughton in 1921. He was marketed as the 'King of Thrillers' and they gave him the trademark image of a trilby, a cigarette holder and a yellow Rolls Royce. He was truly prolific, capable not only of producing a 70,000 word novel in three days but of doing three novels in a row in such a manner. It was estimated that by 1928 one in four books being read was written by Wallace, for alongside his famous thrillers he wrote variously in other genres, including science fiction, non-fiction accounts of WWI which amounted to ten volumes and screen plays. Eventually he would reach the remarkable total of 170 novels, 18 stage plays and 957 short stories.

Wallace became chairman of the Press Club which to this day holds an annual Edgar Wallace Award, rewarding 'excellence in writing'.

Diagnosed with diabetes his health deteriorated and he soon entered a coma and died of his condition and double pneumonia on the 7th of February 1932 in North Maple Drive, Beverly Hills. He was buried near his home in England at Chalklands, Bourne End, in Buckinghamshire.

Index of Contents

INTRODUCING MAJOR HAYNES

Major Haynes readers will recognise as the brilliant British Secret Service man who figured so prominently in the memoirs of Hermann Gallwitz, the German spy, which concluded in our last issue. From the notes of Captain Dane, Hayne's chief of staff, Mr. Wallace has been able to compile a new series of articles dealing with episodes in the Major's amazing career.

Major Hiram Haynes has a standing order with his bookseller, to supply him with all the spy stories that are published, whether in book form or in the current magazines. He says that if he were deprived of the recreation which this form of literature supplies, life would be insupportable and the war an unrelieved tragedy. It is hard to tell how far this statement can be taken seriously.

There is this difficulty in writing of a man who is still living, that on the one hand the biographer lives in terror of offending his subject by overpraise or by ascribing to him motives which were not his, and on the other by avoiding (from a sense of delicacy) certain vital phases of his career and in this way failing to raise one's narrative above the commonplace.

Major Haynes is this kind of man:

He was travelling through Mexico in '12 when his train was held up by a number of ragged gentlemen who represented the official opposition to the Mexican Government. In appearance and method they did not greatly differ from common or garden bandits.

Now it is a known fact which has been recorded by the very greatest of story-writers, that railway passengers in the presence of armed robbers are so many sheep and in the case now cited, they showed no improvement upon their accustomed meekness.

A general or a colonel or maybe a common Mexican insurgent came strolling up the aisle fondling a large revolver and relieved the passengers of their valuables with the nonchalance of a car conductor collecting tickets.

"Hasten," growled the collector of booty, "money—everything!"

Hiram Haynes still smiled and the annoyed Mexican spat at him.

"I do not like your habit," said Haynes in Spanish and shot him through the mouth.

Thereafter was one small war which ended when the last of the bandits galloped to the cover of a distant arroyo and potted the departing train—without injury to any of its scared freight—until it was out of sight.

There was another South American affair.

In a state which shall be nameless there was a certain Pietro Seccecci (pronounced, I think, "Say-checky") who was the proprietor of a large establishment which was called a music hall but was infinitely less innocent.

To this establishment came by almost every boat one or two inexperienced girls who had accepted "theatrical engagements" at promising salaries.

Their disillusionment came soon after their arrival. The place was a crying scandal and the British Consul had unsuccessfully endeavoured to move the authorities to action. But Pietro had a "pull" and no steps were taken against him.

Then Haynes drifted into the town, dined with the consul and heard the story.

"It is horrible," said the consul, "week after week I get girls here—poor little beggars, they are frantic with terror. They are generally in debt to Seccecci who threatens—"

"I know," said Haynes, "my dear consul, I know the story backward—when does the Merrimas Chief clear?"

The consul was surprised at the brusqueness of the question. What had the sailing of an American tramp steamer to do with the plight of stage-struck girls in Queer Street?

"At daybreak—she has her papers. Why do you ask—do you know her skipper?"

"I'm going along to get acquainted," said Haynes. "By-the-way, I am leaving by the midnight for New Orleans."

At two o'clock in the morning, two hours after the northern express had pulled out, a man with a heavy black moustache and wearing spectacles, stalked into the over-heated music room of Seccecci's magnificent Concert-Café (it was called The Pallacio something-or-other) and made his way to where the stout proprietor, resplendent in evening dress and blazing with diamonds, sat.

"Señor," he said loudly, "I am the brother of a girl you have treated abominably."

Seccecci had treated so many girls abominably that he was bewildered by the accusation. Never before had brothers, with or without a knowledge of Spanish, penetrated into the Pallacio and created a scene.

He reached stealthily for his hip pocket but before his gun was out he was a dead man.

The story of that "vile assassination of our eminent and illustrious fellow citizen" will be found in the Diaro de —. Here you may read how the outraged brother leapt through a window and outdistancing his pursuers, disappeared in the neighbourhood of the docks. The Merriraas Chief sailed at dawn and the British Consul wisely held his tongue.

Haynes was a born gun-man. He was a proof that there is truth in the trite admonitions which judges so often deliver to the men they are sending down to durance, that had they employed their ingenuity and courage in a lawful occupation they might have hit the roof.

Haynes was a person, engaged in lawful business, who employed unlawful methods. No conjurer produced a rabbit from a plug hat with greater rapidity than he could conjure from the air the lethal weapon, in the use of which he was so great an artist. He stretched out an empty hand—presto! something was in it—something black and shiny and menacing.

In 1911 when Germany and France were on the brink of war over the question of the Agadir, an innocent tourist, armed with a butterfly net went out of Liège toward the German border. An hour later he was being shown out of one of the forts—it was Chaudfontein—by a polite Belgian non-commissioned officer who accepted his explanation that he had climbed the forbidden glacis in search of a paphia glycerium or some member of the order Rhopalocera.

He wandered on to Visé and sent a telegram to a certain address in Paris. It was a telegram which dealt with the health of his aunt. It was a very long telegram and it described her symptoms in detail.

Officials at the Quai d'Orsay read it with interest and a 'phone call was put through to Brussels. The conversation was mainly about guns which ought to have been mounted and were not mounted. A colonel was retired, a minister was dismissed, but long before this happened, the tourist with the butterfly net was in a nursing home recovering from the effects of an artfully poisoned vol-au-vent, which had been served to him at Aix-la-Chapelle. For the German secret police knew him and when the station master's office was burgled at Aix and the secret mobilization instructions disappeared they arranged his funeral and provided almost everything but the corpse.

Haynes was half dying when he was smuggled across the frontier by a clever young man named Dane—whose name will appear in this record—and for three weeks he hovered (as the sentimental writers say) between life and death

"This is a lesson to me," he said to his chief. "I guess I'll give it up."

"The service?" demanded his superior In some concern.

"No—vol-au-vent," said Haynes.

After his convalescence he took three weeks' leave and went back to Aix—for he was, as I say, a born gun-man with all a gun-man's poetical sense of justice.

From the Kölner Zeitung of 21st December 1911 I clip the following:

"Yesterday evening Franz Helle, employed as waiter at the Kölner Hof, was the victim of a strange outrage. The unfortunate man, who until recently was employed at the Hôtel Heullens at Aachen (Aix-la-Chapelle) was returning at 1 a.m. from Bahnhof Straat to his home in Duetz when he was accosted by a stranger who held him at the mouth of a pistol and compelled him to eat twenty noxious pastries. Helle, who is now lying dangerously ill in the Burger Hospital, states that his assailant was an Englishman or American who had been taken ill after being served by Helle at Aachen and that the miscreant is a dangerous spy. The police are pursuing enquiries."

That is the sort of man Haynes is.

For what government he worked in pre-war days nobody knew. It was his boast to Dane—the only man admitted to his confidence—that he had been publicly repudiated by every one except Liberia. In 1911 he was undoubtedly working for the Second Bureau of the French Ministry of War. In 1910 he was as certainly at the end of a wire which stretched from Pekin to Washington. In the early part of the war he fought with the Legion d'Estranges in France and later was liaison officer between the Belgian and the British Armies.

In 1915-16 he was at a desk in the British War Office with the rank of Major. A good-looking lean-faced man inclined to sallowness, he conveyed an impression of slightness of build which was somewhat deceptive.

The British found him a veritable encycloaedia of political crime. He knew every anarchist leader there was in the world and had graded them in their order of frightfulness. His acquaintanceship ranged from Grand Dukes to confidence men. (Imagine if you can the fit of apoplexy which all but overcame the Bishop of Panton when, bearing off the Major to luncheon, the pair were accosted by a man in a noisy suit who addressed his companion as "Hi" and, answering Haynes' enquiry, admitted unblushingly that he had just been released from prison after a two-year sentence for fraud).

He spoke seven modern languages and read two dead ones, could and did quote Browning with remarkable fidelity, could live for a week without sleep, wrote the most villainous hand that any War Office clerk had ever deciphered—but first and best of all his accomplishments he was the compleat gun-man.

Fearless and unconventional in his methods, possessed of astounding coolness and audacity and a quaint sense of humour, Major Hiram Haynes has become the terror of enemy agents all over the world.

The first of his adventures appears below.

CHAPTER I

MAJOR HAYNES AND THE PRINCESS

Between them on a dwarf table was a tray containing coffee and liqueurs. Haynes, who was one of the two, was smoking a cigarette through a long amber holder; his companion, a tall, thick-set civilian, keen-eyed, alert, and impressively capable-looking, smoked a cigar.

"You certainly look dandy in that uniform, Hi," said the guest approvingly.

Chief Healy, of the newly-created C.E. Branch of the U.S. Intelligence Bureau, had a sense of humour.

"I feel safer with you in that kit," he nodded; "it kind of settles you in my mind. I hate to tell you so, but I have always accepted you with reservations—there's a grand criminal lost in you."

"Quite right," agreed the other lazily; "that is why I hold my job, and that is probably the reason you hold yours. Counter-espionage work calls for the illegal mind. That is where some of our people—and yours—go wrong. They put a man on to a clever devil who spends five-sixths of his time preparing alibis, and they wonder why patient investigation produces no other evidence than that when the crime was committed at 7.30 p.m. in Paris the accused was seen playing patience in Biarritz. You know the type—absolutely unconvictable."

Healy nodded again.

"Here's a case in point which will interest you," Haynes went on, and drawing a flat leather case from the pocket of his uniform jacket he laid it open upon the table. "Do you know that lady?"

The case contained the portrait of a girl. It was a beautiful face that Healy viewed. There was a delicacy in its moulding and a wide-eyed innocence in its expression that was disarming. The little portrait case was fitted for two photographs, but in the second space, facing the picture, was a sheet of stiff paper covered with figures in a microscopic hand.

"A code?" asked Healy looking up.

"Hardly," smiled the other, "no cipher above a nine. Note how every figure is equidistant from the other, and how even ones occupy as much space as the eights. A work of care, eh? Now, take a pencil and draw a line from the first of the nines to the nearest four—you needn't worry about disfiguring the card, it is a photographic reproduction. Go from 9 to 4, from 4 to 9, and continue."

He watched the chief's pencil moving amidst the figures.

"Phew!" cried Healy suddenly. "Why, this is a drawing of a gun."

"Of the new Whelt mortar," said Haynes: "clever, isn't it? That lady is the Princess Sabochiffski, the daughter of a high Russian official, and was until a month ago occupying one of the best suites at the best hotel in London."

"Wasn't that enough?"

"Not on your life." Haynes shook his head. "In the first place the card was not found in the lady's possession. It was discovered in the post—just a postal picture view of the Houses of Parliament. You know the method of 'detection'?"

"Sure. Take one well-nourished postcard, steam slowly over alcohol until the edges gape, carefully strip picture until the writing is revealed, and serve the sender hot."

"There's a chef lost in you, Jim," laughed Haynes. "Well—there it is. The postcard is traced to the Princess—of course, we have no direct proof. This isn't a job for a flat-footed policeman with a notebook. You can't do any of that grand spying work that you read about in exciting fiction."

Healy rolled his cigar from one corner of his mouth to the other and chuckled.

"A masked figure rubbering secret drawers? No, I guess that's out. What did you do?"

"It was absurdly simple. One of the aviation people offered to take her for a flight—the lady is keen on that sort of thing. Took her out to sea—lost his bearings—forced landing in Holland—apologies to the lady—machine and aviator interned. Cost, about two thousand and the temporary loss of a man, but it saved complications."

"She tried to get back?"

"Sure thing—but there were passport difficulties. The lady's relatives were furious, but what would you do? Passport difficulties are the common lot in 'these iron times.' God bless the German for the phrase."

He beckoned a club waiter and paid his bill.

"Where now?" asked Healy.

"Home—gentle recreation—sleep," said Haynes.

"Fine—I'm going along to your Scotland Yard. I've got to fit things in if I am to sail by Thursday."

A waiter came toward them carrying a letter.

"For me?" asked Major Haynes.

He picked up the envelope and glanced at its flap.

"Hotel Astoria—good lord!"

He tore open the envelope and extracted a letter, read it in silence, and handed it to his companion.

Jim Healy fixed his glasses and read:—

Dear Major Haynes,

You will be surprised to receive this! Such a strange thing happened. As you know, I was at the Hague till this morning through some stupid trouble about my passport. This morning Mr. Van John very kindly took me on a trip in his airplane, and just the same thing happened as happened a month ago. We got lost in the mist and made a forced landing in Essex! Am I not unfortunate, and won't you please come along and see me?

Sincerely yours,

Olga Sabochiffski.

They looked at one another, and Haynes was the first to grin.

"Well, what do you know about that?" asked Healy in a tone of admiration. "That dame has left you no alternative, Hi—you'll have to bounce or be bounced. You didn't tell me you were on calling terms."

"I'm not," said Haynes quietly; "that's the queer thing about it. I've never met her or corresponded with her. I was under the impression that she was unaware of my existence—so far as her deportation was concerned. She's been busy in Holland, and Berlin has put her wise. This is a challenge."

He flourished the letter, and a bright light shone in his eyes.

The two men walked out of the club together, and parted at the corner of Brook Street.

"If I were you," said Healy at parting, "I'd go along to the Minister of the Interior or the Lord High State Secretary, or whoever is the guy responsible, and I'd get a repatriation order and fix her straight away."

Haynes shook his head.

"The cave-man system of diplomacy doesn't go with a first cousin to the Czarina and the niece of the Russian Minister of War," he said. "I'm going along to see Olga."

He hailed a taxi and drove, first to his flat, depositing the flat leather case in a place of security. Then he sat down in his dark study and thought. Here was a girl engaged in espionage work of a particularly dangerous character. She was admitted to the best and most exclusive naval and military circles, she was very beautiful, and she was extremely clever.

He changed his mind about interviewing his superior, and drove to the private residence of a permanent Secretary to the Home Office, being at once admitted to the presence of that great man. The old official listened to the brief narration, and when Haynes had finished stretched back in his chair and shook his head.

"The position with regard to Russia is too volatile. We pretty well know that the Government is letting us down, and I agree with you that this girl is probably working for Germany. Branstoff knows it, but is helpless. We cannot afford to antagonise further certain people in the Czarina's entourage, and a deportation order would, in all probability, lead to such a breach. Take any course you wish, but I warn you that the Government will, if expedient, repudiate any action of yours which you may take. The girl is known to be a pro-German—even the Russian Court has protested to her cousin and uncle."

"But why—she's a pure Russian?"

The Secretary shrugged his shoulders.

"I don't understand women—do you?"

"Like a book," said Major Haynes arrogantly.

He had no settled plan in his mind when he was ushered into the private sitting-room of Princess Sabochiffski.

A slight figure rose from a settee to give him a smiling welcome. She was undeniably lovely. The face was perfect of its type. ("Her eyes alone were worth a pilgrimage," he wrote to Healy). And there was in her every movement a charm most delicate and rare.

"Major Haynes?" she said. "I'm so glad you came—I wanted to see you dreadfully."

"And here I am, Princess, in my most dreadful and sinister aspect," he laughed as he took her hand.

She looked him fearlessly in the eyes.

"You're not so dreadful as I thought you would be," she said quietly. "As a rule I hate meeting clever men—they are so disappointing."

She pushed a low easy chair forward, and with a little bow he placed it in position—but not the position she had chosen.

"You do not like to sit with your back to a door, of course," she laughed. "You prefer your back to a window—even though there is a fire-escape balcony outside, and you might be as easily shot from there as from my bedroom—ah! I see you think I am really dangerous."

("Her laughter was like a peal of silver bells, believe me," wrote the irrepressible Haynes.)

"In a sense I think you are, Princess," he said gallantly, "but since we have drifted into frankness, I may say that I shifted the position of my chair in order that I might see you better."

She settled herself in one corner of the deep couch, and folding her arms across its end faced him.

"You wonder why I sent for you," she said, "bravado, you think—no, that is not it. Possibly I have made a mistake in asking you to come—I have just a little nervous feeling that I have been imprudent. You wish me to tell you something about myself? No? Well, you know it all, yes?"

"First at the beginning," she went on, never taking her eyes off him, "I was educated in Germany."

"At the Akademie of Frau Stephan, Bismarck Strasse, Karlsruhe," murmured Haynes, and there was a glint of amusement in the girl's fine eyes.

"I see—you have my dossier. Tell me, then, where shall I begin? I lived in Berlin up to the beginning of the war, when I went to Petrograd. There I remained until December, 1915—you see, I wish to inform you."

Haynes nodded.

"In that case you will satisfy my curiosity to this extent. Why, in December, 1914, did you go to Stockholm, staying there for three weeks? Why, in the period you say you remained in Russia, did you make four trips to Holland, travelling under the name of Madame Livoff?"

He did not expect that she would show any sign of embarrassment—he was surprised that she did. A faint flush came to her face and she jerked up her chin.

"That was no affair of—of Governments," she said with a touch of hauteur, "who told you such—such an absurd story? What is it that you know or think you know?"

All her self-possession, all the light pleasantry was gone. Her voice was hard, almost metallic, and her curious little faults of speech were accentuated.

Haines was alert, noting every phase of a situation which had undergone so singular a change.

"I know nothing," he said blandly, "except that such visits were paid, that you stayed with the widow of Junkheer van Reeden, and that for six months of 1916 you were untraceable, even as the guest of Madame van Reeden."

She was looking at him steadily, searchingly, and evidently her search satisfied her, for her manner became more composed.

"That fact is public property," she said carelessly. "I was coming to that; my relatives were alarmed by my disappearance, and I suppose that you, as well as every other policeman—"

"Say 'copper,'" urged Haynes, "it sounds more homely."

She frowned.

"Copper? Oh, yes, that is slang, is it not? I went away because I was tired of the war. I was in the Convent of the Sacred Heart at the Hague—the guest of the good Mother Superior. There is no mystery about that."

There was a ring of defiance in her voice.

"None at all," said the suave Haynes.

"Are you satisfied?"

"About what, Princess?"

"That I am not—not a dangerous person to be forcibly deported because you are so afraid of my powerful relations that you dare not eject me by legal means."

Major Haynes spread out his hands in a gesture of protest, and the girl laughed again.

"You think I am a spy, my dear Major Haynes? Is there anything I could learn from my friends more valuable than the information that your indiscreet newspapers reveal?"

She rose quickly and walked across the room to a table near the door where a small bundle of evening "specials" were lying.

"I will show you how clever men discover secrets," she rallied him as she opened one of the papers; "it is so simple—there is no need for spies. You reveal your secrets unconsciously. Look, here is a notice of a theatrical slump. 'There is a dearth of khaki, in the theatres,' says the writer. That means all army leave is stopped and that your offensive is near, is it not so? Here is another that says—"

She stopped, and Haynes, watching her, saw her face turn white.

"My God!" she whispered. "Oh, my God!"

He was on his feet in a second.

"Princess, is there anything—"

She dropped the paper and flung out her hands.

"Keep away—keep away!" her eyes were blazing with fury and now she was speaking in German. "I hate you—I hate you and your country! May God punish you!"

He was silent before the concentrated agony in her voice.

"You think I am dangerous—expel me! I am—bitterly dangerous. Tell your masters that I will work to ruin you and your degenerate Allies. Hear me! I will work till I die—I will—"

She swayed and fell back upon the sofa.

"Go away—go away—send my maid."

Haynes bowed and left the room, kicking the fallen newspaper before him as he went.

Outside the room he stooped and picked it up and pushed it into his pocket before he pressed one of the corridor bells and sent the chambermaid, who came in answer to the summons, in search of the Princess' maid.

Twenty minutes later he was in his study, carefully scrutinising the page which had produced so dramatic and crushing an effect upon the self-possessed member of the Russian aristocracy.

There was a resumé of Parliament—nothing in that. A ship had gone ashore off the North Foreland, and was reported a total wreck—nothing or, possibly little in that. A divorce case of a conventional kind—he read the evidence carefully, despising no possibility, but the parties were suburban tradespeople. So he went down each column until he found tucked away under the heading, "News in Brief" the following paragraph:—

"A Reuter wire from Amsterdam announces the death in action of Lt. Baron von Keller, whose name appeared in the German communique of last Friday as having brought down his twentieth enemy machine in air-fighting. He was shot down by a British airman."

Haynes searched the paper again, and one by one rejected every other story in favour of this.

He called up a certain information bureau in Whitehall.

"Who is von Keller—Baron von Keller?" he asked. "I know half a dozen—yes, the airman. What is his age and history?"

He waited with the receiver at his ear, and presently he picked up a pencil.

"Yes?" he said as he wrote. "Secretary of Legation—at Stockholm in 1914? Yes. At the Hague in 1915? Joined the Flying Corps in 1916. Anything else? Where is his home? Karlsruhe? Thank you."

He hung up the receiver, and spent the greater part of the night coding telegrams addressed to Stockholm, The Hague, and Petrograd.

He was roused from a brief sleep at ten o'clock the following morning by an urgent 'phone message.

"Will you please come right away to the office," said the voice of his assistant. "There's trouble."

He dressed, and without stopping to breakfast hurried to the little room at the War Office, the four walls of which were plastered with secrets.

"What's wrong—don't tell me that the War Office has been burgled by a veiled woman and the plans of the new offensive stolen?" he said flippantly. "You have awakened me from my beauty sleep, Dane— justify yourself."

Dane never smiled. He was a solemn-faced young man with a limp. He was indeed the most serious thing that Haynes had ever met with. Not that he was gloomy; on the contrary, he was an optimist with reservations. He took the world and his work seriously. He took Haynes seriously, but he took himself most seriously of all.

"I often wish, sir," he said, "that you would not speak of espionage—"

"Cut out that sadness," said Haynes "What is wrong?"

For answer Dane laid a telegram before his chief.

It was from Madrid, and beneath the inconsequent and meaningless code was written, in Dane's boyish hand, the translation: —

"Chart of new minefield north of Shetland in enemy's hands. Tracing shown by German Admiralty to Marquis de Boussa at three this morning."

"I've been over to the Admiralty," said Dane. "They say that the chart was not completed until the day before yesterday, and that if the Imperial German Government has it, it must have been sent by direction code last night."

Major Haynes sat down at his desk and scratched his unshaven chin thoughtfully.

"H'm," he said, "quick work. De Boussa is a close friend of von Capelle's chief of staff. I suppose de Boussa (strafe him for a German!) had to send the good news to his brother, the Bishop, and that is how our man got it—but how did she get the information?"

"She, sir?" asked Dane more soberly than ever. "Was it a lady?"

"A perfect lady," said Haynes grimly, for in his own mind he was quite convinced that this was more of the Princess's work.

That night there was an air raid on London, and Haynes, standing in the deserted street watching the shrapnel bursting in the sky, had a narrow escape. It is true that no bomb fell nearer than two miles from him, and that no anti-aircraft shrapnel or shell base was discovered in the roadway.

The two bullets which fanned his face came from the street level. He did not even hear the pistol fired, because the antiaircraft guns were putting up a particularly noisy barrage, and the shots were drowned in the noise of their explosions. But he felt the wind of the bullets, and heard them thud against the door behind him. He saw only the disappearing tail light of a taxi, and knew that there was no profit in pursuit, though he was tempted to take a long shot at the taxi.

The next day he was stopped in Piccadilly by a woman of a peculiarly unpleasant character, who threw her arms about his neck and called him "Hiram." A raw Assistant Provost Marshal who had been manœuvred to the spot took his name, but Haynes arrested the woman, and by a system of cross-examination which is not usually permitted discovered that she had been paid for her work by an East End Russian with a German name.

All the time answers were coming to his telegraphed inquiries, and they were satisfactory.

On the third night following his interview with Princess Olga Sabochiffski he was called to an important war conference at the Ministry of War Measures.

"This is the position, Haynes," said the harassed Minister. "The Princess has accepted an invitation from Admiral — to visit a port where certain preparations are in progress which we are most anxious should not become known. We have conveyed a hint to the Admiral, and he is furious and demands an explanation. If we forbid the visit he will resign, and questions will be asked in the House of Commons. It seems to me that we might as well deport the lady and get the trouble over, but the Cabinet doesn't want that to happen."

"I will settle with the Princess tonight," said Major Haynes confidently.

He was leaving the room when the Minister called him back.

"Oh, by the way, I have news of that person you were inquiring about," he said, and gave certain particulars.

"This," said Haynes as he left, "is where I score ten."

The last telegram he was awaiting reached him before he left his flat that night. It contained one word, "Sailed." and the face of Major Haynes was one big smile.

He drove to the Astoria and sent up his card and was received by the Princess.

She looked paler than when he had seen her before, a little finer drawn. She gave him no smile, nor did she offer him any of those delightful courtesies which had marked his first visit.

"I can give you five minutes, Major Haynes," she said, sitting bolt upright on the edge of an armchair, her hands folded in her lap.

"Quite long enough," said Haynes cheerfully "I shall not ask for longer—though if you press me I will stay."

"What is your business?" she asked.

"There is a train which connects with the Hook of Holland packet," said Haynes slowly. "It leaves London at 8.30 to-morrow, and you will travel by it."

She smiled disdainfully.

"I am permitted to telegraph to the Czarina and my uncle that I am deported?" she asked.

"Surely, but if you do I shall also wire."

"To say?"

She raised her eyebrows.

"To say," said Haynes quietly, "that you are the Baroness von Keller, that you were secretly married to von Keller in the Chapel of the Sacred Heart, and that a child was born of that marriage during the six months you vanished from your agonised relatives."

She was on her feet, white to the lips.

"I—I have done nothing I am ashamed of," she said with unnatural calm. "I married—where my heart was. You shall not blackmail me."

Major Haynes bowed.

"You will leave by the 8.30 for three reasons. The first, is that you are a German subject; the second is that I have your son in safe keeping—"

She had half-turned, but now she swung round on him, her eyes blazing.

"You lie—you lie! He is in Holland!"

"Was," corrected the other. "He was taken from Madame van Reeden by one of my agents, and at this moment is at Harwich."

She tried to speak, but could not. The delicate face was drawn and haggard.

"You have won," she said at last in a low voice, "but how cowardly—a child—"

"I was a child once," said Haynes sentimentally, "a bonnie little boy with curls. That did not prevent your good friends from trying to pot me from a taxi, nor your agents from endeavouring to blacken by means of a depraved woman my unstained character. All's fair in war. You will go?"

She nodded, not raising her eyes from the carpet.

"Nothing matters much—now," she said sadly, "except the boy."

He looked at her.

"Have you received any communications lately from your friends in Germany?"

She shook her head.

"You have seen to that," she replied.

"How many Von Kellers are there in the German Army?" he asked.

She looked up quickly.

"What do you mean?" she gasped.

"Only that the Von Keller who was killed is not your husband, but his cousin."

She reeled, and he caught her.

"You—you mean that?" she whispered.

"Your husband has been returned to the Diplomatic service—but, lord," he checked himself, "I'm actually giving information to the enemy!"

The old smile was in her eyes when she put out her hand to him.

"I will catch that 8.30 train," she said.

"And I'll be there to see you off," said Major Haynes, "both officially and unofficially."

CHAPTER II

THE MISSING HOHENZOLLERN

Depicting what all of us will applaud when it comes to the disposition of the reigning house of the German Empire.

WHEN the war broke out the cadets of the House of Hohenzollern were assigned their various duties. Prince Max went into the army and commanded a brigade, Prince Charles Frederick rejoined the Death's Head Hussars, and Prince Adolph went into the Intelligence Bureau of the German Foreign Office, and found himself in consequence doomed to obscurity until the great idea came to him. Whereupon he sought his august relative.

Prince Adolph was urgent, plausible, talked of singeing the King of Spain's beard, and the Head of the house, with many admonitions, cautions, warnings, and the like, consented, and Prince Adolph disappeared from Berlin society—and, strangely enough, has not been heard of since.

Three months later Major Haynes, of the Counter-Espionage Bureau, was disposing of a very troublesome personage against whom no very special evidence was available.

This person was the redoubtable Corbori, who was by nature lawless, and by inclination an Anarchist. A deportation order had been made against him, but an unexpected difficulty arose. The country of Corbori's birth, on learning that it was intended to ship him to the dear homeland, sent an urgent request that the deportation should be made to some other land.

"I'm worried sick over this man Corbori," said the chief to Haynes. "You're an ingenious and unscrupulous man—can't you think up something?"

Haynes rolled his cigar between his teeth and looked out of the window.

"The Government send a mail to Tristan d'Acuna every two years," he said. "There are about three hundred people on the island, and no boats call. This year the mail goes by sailing ship, the Palagonia, and the voyage will take six months. Why not send him to Tristan d'Acuna?"

"Rather, tough on Tristan d'Acuna, isn't it? How will you explain the dumping of a speech-making Anarchist to the good islanders?"

"Tell 'em it's war work," said Haynes.

He could not give much attention to the matter because he had his own worries. He was interviewing his police all that day over a very ingenious plan which he had unearthed to secure the escape of a political prisoner, but he interviewed also the master of the Palagonia, who wore a Derby hat and chewed tobacco, and wanted exact information as to the amount of food the doomed Corbori would consume.

"We go down on the ebb tide tomorrow morning," said the skipper. "Better get this Corb—whatever his blinking name is—on board a little before daylight. How much do I get for carrying him?"

Haynes named a sum, and the skipper chewed furiously.

"I'll take a dozen at that price," he said. Haynes showed him out of his office, and opened the window to clear the room of the smell of the sea, which is tobacco, tar, oilskin, and other death-defying odours.

Then he went home, for he had a dinner engagement which promised to be unusually interesting. At ten o'clock that night he sat in a pleasant room in company which, at least, was entertaining.

You might describe the room and its appointments as most elegant without exaggerating in the least. It was one of those luxurious saloons which are so unexpectedly found behind the unpromising facades of such London houses as you find in Berkeley or Grosvenor Squares.

The furniture was Louis Quinze, with the exception of the big baize-covered card-table and the five stuffed chairs which surrounded it. In one corner of the room was a great glass cabinet, its shelves covered with miniatures in rich settings, the curtains were of corded silk, the walls were panelled with veritable tapestries of the 14th century, and all that was jarringly modern was the Jacobean buffet with its array of bottles, glasses, and silver ware, the shaded extension lamp over the card table, and the table itself.

If the room, with lazy red fire and red, shaded lamp, its soft shadows (for there was no other light save that above the table) carried a sense of comfort on a night when a north-westerly gate was howling through the streets of London, and sending rain in sheets against the shuttered windows, the company was as comfortable. The stout, bald man in evening dress stood for opulence. The bearded exquisite who lolled back in one of the chairs critically examining the glass of wine he held stood for refinement and wealth, the hatchet-faced man with the old-fashioned shoe-string cravat was conservative finance, the bull-necked man with the bristling moustache and the rough hands was rugged success. As for the fifth man he might be anything, for he wore an army uniform innocent of decoration.

"Major Haynes isn't drinking. Open some Perrier Jouet, Frank."

Major Haynes did not protest. He was smiling as at the remembrance of some rare jest, and idly fingering the little pile of bank notes at his right hand. He took the wine when it came without looking at it, and emptied the glass without setting it down.

"It is interesting to get your views," he said after a while. "As I understand them they amount to this— that opportunity is the mother of fortune."

The bull-necked man laughed shortly.

"I should say so," he said, "seizing opportunity gave me a million kronen, and in the first weeks of the war."

"I often think," said the Exquisite, looking up at the ceiling, "that fortunes are so easily made that it is a crime, not to be poor, but to be moderately rich. Now you, Major Haynes. Are, I suppose, a well-off man? Good. You will probably be a well-off man all your life. Good again. You will have enough to buy a fruit farm in California or take your annual holiday on the Riviera or winter at Palm Beach. But you must always enjoy life within the limits of a limited income. You cannot obey your whims. You cannot keep your yacht. You are disciplined, and must fall into line at the ticket office, at the steamer's gangway, wherever being one of the crowd compels you to queue up."

"Will you kindly give me the recipe for fortune-making?" asked Haynes good-humouredly.

"Opportunity," said four voices at once, and Mr Hamlyn von Koos, that elegant Hollander, laughed.

"Neutral opinion is unanimous," he quoted, "and here speak four voices of international wisdom, Major—Sweden, Denmark, Switzerland, and may I add Holland? Opportunity! Every one of us owe our fortunes to different causes. Mr. Vieille,"—he indicated the hatchet-faced man, "founded his fortune at Monte Carlo. Mr. Onderson,"—he nodded toward the bald man, "speculated in oil. Mr. Gustave,"—the bull-necked man smiled self-consciously,—"jumped into the rubber market at the right moment and made his escape with a fortune whilst I, who inherited money, more than doubled my capital the year that Ajax won the Grand Prix of Paris."

He saw the twitch on the major's lips and laughed again.

"Now, I'm sure you're amused at the turn the conversation has taken," he said. "Confess that when I invited you to meet a few neutral friends you expected we should—what is the word?—pump you? Yes, pump you so that you told us some of your precious military secrets. And we talk only of money—and what is more, you win ours!"

He stretched out his hands and took up the cards, shuffled them deftly and with a "my deal I think," dealt them out.

The game was poker, which Major Haynes had preferred to baccarat, and it was interesting. Quite a respectable pile of notes had accumulated at his corner of the table since they had sat down.

The game progressed uneventfully for the greater part of an hour. At the end of that time the betting rose to sums which would have made the average man gasp to hear. Haynes heard without gasping. He just threw in his hands and watched the play. He saw ten thousand pounds pass on two pairs; was an interested spectator to a brisk three-cornered duel in which some £15,000 was involved, and saw the big stakes go to the bland Mr. Onderson on a sheer bluff, and then the silent-footed manservant produced another magnum. A new hand was dealt and he picked up four aces and began to take notice. Now four aces are pretty nearly as good a hand as a man can draw at poker. Only a straight flush can beat it and the chances of a straight flush being out against "fours" is about one in twenty thousand.

Haynes looked at his hand thoughtfully as Mr. Onderson gave a little grunt.

"I haf a most excellent hand,"' he said with his bland smile, "and this time Mr. Van Koos—I take off all limits."

"That is strange," said the elegant Hollander. I also have an excellent hand and I will accompany you to the roof—it is a thousand to play, I believe," he added, pushing forward a slip of paper and scribbling a sum and his initials. "It is now two thousand. Are you in this, major?"

"Up to the skies," said Haynes, and wrote his I.O.U.

They drew cards, Haynes discarding his useless card as a matter of form. He looked at his cards again and held them for a moment in the palm of his hand and laid them face downward on the table.

And then the betting started. At twenty thousand Vieille dropped out. At thirty thousand Haynes hesitated.

"It is very absurd betting in these terrific sums—I am not a rich man."

Mr. Van Koos laid down his cards.

"Major Haynes," he said earnestly, "this may be your opportunity. If you win, you win a fortune, if you lose I will take your note of hand—there is only you and I left in the game."

But Haynes still hesitated,

"Go the limit," urged the other.

"I will make it forty thousand pounds," said Haynes.

"At which price I will see you, for I realize that I have you beaten," smiled Mr. Van Koos, and laid down the knave, ten, nine, eight and seven of diamonds—as pleasing a little straight flush as any player could hope to hold against four aces.

Haynes did not speak.

He just laid down his cards—a straight flush to the ace.

"My coup, I think," he said.

For a moment there was a tense silence, then Van Koos leaped up, his face livid.

"You—you cheat!" he spluttered, "you had four aces!"

He stopped suddenly, recognizing his appalling blunder.

"How did you know?" asked Haynes quietly, "because you fixed the deck? Stand where you are, Onderson!"

He covered the bald man with an unexpected Browning.

"Just where you are, dear lad—put your hands where I can see them,"

He swept the money from his corner of the table into his pocket.

"Fair winnings, I think—I saw where the game went crooked—after your aged servitor brought the drinks and palmed you the new deck."

"I suppose you consider yourself an officer and a gentleman," sneered Van Koos, very white now, "you are invited to a gentleman's house to play cards and you cheat—eh? That is a nice word for your superior officer —eh?"

"I only know one better one," said Haynes cordially.

"You take our money—you accept our hospitality—you drink our wine—"

"Very excellent wine, too," murmured Haynes, fondling his Browning.

"And threaten to shoot us because we detect you."

Haynes was still seated, and now he nodded to the chair which his host had vacated.

"Sit down," he commanded, "and listen to a little homely truth. You asked me here to skin me—swindle me, if you understand that better. You lured me on with your fine talk of 'opportunity,' and it was your object to get me so in your debt that I would convey a letter to a man called Thion, who is now awaiting trial in the Tower on a charge of espionage—don't faint, there's worse to come. With the object of effecting his escape before or after his trial, a most elaborate scheme has been arranged—and it is necessary that he should be made acquainted with the particulars of the plan. Therefore the letter."

"I think, Major, you have made a mistake," faltered van Koos.

His face was ghastly, and the hand that stroked his beard was shaking like a leaf.

"I never make that kind of mistake," said Haynes quietly. "Now I am going to make an offer to you. Tell me frankly why you are taking so much trouble and are prepared to spend so much money to effect the escape of a fairly insignificant spy, who, I can assure you, has learnt nothing of our secrets, since he has been under observation from the moment he arrived in England, and I will save his life—and possibly yours, though this I will not promise. You get me here, and think you're going to do just what makes you gladdest, and you start squealing because you can't get away with your funny business. By the Lord, you'll be sorry you ever met me before I'm through."

There was nothing gentle about Major Haynes now. His voice had the bullying, hectoring tone of the police official, purposely designed to silence and cow. It had another purpose. He stalked from the room, and the serving man made to open the door for him.

"I don't want your assistance, Benson," he said, and the man started back as if he had been shot, for he had been called by the name he had been sentenced under in 1899 to ten years for forgery and impersonation.

The men in the room were silent till they heard the clang of the front door.

"Go down and see which way he went, Frank," said van Koos quickly. "See if he has somebody watching outside."

Benson disappeared, and came back in a few minutes.

"Gone," he said curtly, and he spoke as an equal. "He had a car waiting, I expect. Well, you've made a mess of it, Hendrich. What will von Bissen say when he comes?"

"Von Bissen should have been here—it was his idea—"

"What shall we do?" asked van Koos.

"Beat it," said the "servant" laconically as he helped himself to a drink, "whilst we're all safe."

"And leave—"

"No names—no names!" mumbled Onderson. "My God, why did he come! What bravado! What madness!"

"There's no sense, in that kind of talk," interrupted the hatchet-faced man. They were speaking in English, the only language apparently which was commonly understood. "He's here, and he must be got away. See here, my friend," he addressed Benson, "there must be no talk of running away. We've engaged you for a big job, with risks, and we've paid a big price. You didn't think that it was a picnic, did you? You can't quit till you're through with it." He looked at his watch. "Von Bissen should be here soon—tell him you're quitting."

"I know when I've had enough," said Benson coolly, "that guy knows me—and I've never been before a judge or as much as pinched in Britain. When you told me he was an English officer I thought it dead easy—that feller's been trained in the States. I'm no quitter, but I've surely got cold feet. He's seen me. He knows me—he'll guess just what I'm here for. It's a pretty idea of yours, but it won't work. I do the job—and then I'm through."

"When is the trial fixed?" asked Vieille.

"Next Monday—Westminster Guildhall—ten o'clock," replied van Koos, sitting, a dejected-looking figure, his elbows on his knees, his chin in his hand. "We've got to do something."

"You'll be lucky to have the chance," sneered Benson. ."You don't think that fellow has gone home to sleep, do you? My advice to you, gentlemen, is to beat it—quick. As far as I am concerned, U-boats or no U-boats, it's me for little old New York, where I know the worst thing that can happen to me."

Onderson, the one man who retained his poise, laughed.

"You'll go when we're ready," he raid. "On Monday the work will be finished—and then, you can leave. Haynes will take no action—he is after a much bigger thing than any of us represent. We'll be shadowed night and day, and the prisoner will be watched."

Benson was idly shuffling the cards, and he did not look up as he spoke.

"There is only one thing for you to do, gentlemen. I'm not in this. Von Bissen asked me to produce an official order for the transfer of the prisoner to Dublin, where he was arrested—I've done my job, all except the date. Yes, sir, official stamp, signature of the Lord Lieutenant, counter signature of the Home Secretary, endorsement of the Officer Commanding the London District—done in duplicate, railway warrants, visiting cards for the detectives who take him away, letters establishing identity—I guess I've done my share. I'll fill in the dates and quit—the rest is your job."

"What are we to do?"

Benson went on shuffling the cards.

"I'm not suggesting anything—but I know just what my old friend Lew Sheffiski (God rest him, he went to the chair two years since) would have done. He'd have reckoned that this fellow Haynes knew a darned sight more than it's healthy for any man to know, and he'd have shot him up."

"Murder—you're mad!" Van Koos was on his feet.

"Benson is right," broke in Onderson roughly, "it's death for us if this man can work a case against us."

He looked round from face to face and found no encouragement.

"I'll do it myself," he said quietly. "Benson is right."

An electric bell shrilled in the basement. "That's von Bissen," said Benson, getting up, "you might find he'll take the job off your hands."

He went out of the room and presently returned with a thick-set man of middle age, whose face was wreathed in smiles.

"Ah, so your policeman fooled you!" he chuckled. "And whilst be fooled you—behold I have fooled the policemen."

He plumped into a chair.

"Wine—the white and the sweet, good Benson. Mein Gott! I am a happy man this night, though we may be all in gaol tomorrow. Gentlemen, our illustrious friend is to be released. A miracle! Consider that Sazanoff is Foreign Minister to the Russian Court—and Sazanoff is implacable and uncorruptible. Yet we got behind him. I never dreamt it was possible, gentlemen—or we would not have taken such trouble. But our prisoner is to be released on the intervention of our good friend the little Czar. To his health!"

He drank the big glass of champagne at a gulp, wiped his moustache, and smiled upon the company.

"To-morrow at a discreet hour we shall take him from the grip of the baffled lion. No need for that ambulance to Cornwall with our prisoner swathed in bandages or the U-boat, eh?"

"And no shooting up," said Mr Onderson, not without relief. "Benson, we must prepare for a search of the house to-night or to-morrow. The best thing you can do is destroy every piece of evidence you have."

Benson nodded, he too had foreseen such a possibility.

"I'll get right away on that," he said, and went up to his room at the top of the house whistling.

It was a large room under the roof, and was plainly furnished. There was a big table with a litter of writing material, vulcanising apparatus, tiny printing forms, magnifying glasses, and tiny bottles. He lit a fire ready laid in the grate, and walked to a cabinet placed between the two windows which gave light to the room. This he opened. Inside were a number of shelves, and these were filled with printed forms. He took them out, gathering them into the crook of his arm, and grinned as he thought of the care which had been shown in their collection.

For these blanks were exact reproductions of confidential forms used by British public departments, and each had been printed in Germany. There were orders for deportation, orders to view public buildings, police warrants, death warrants printed on ivory-coloured parchment, soldiers' and sailors' discharge certificates, blank passports, every authorisation that accompanies ordinary or extraordinary action was here waiting for the expert to fill in the details and affix an awe-inspiring signature.

He laid them on the table, and, unlocking a steel box within the cabinet, took out an official envelope and extracted three or four blue-tinted sheets of foolscap. These he surveyed with the pride of a good craftsman. They were orders of removal addressed to "Our Constable of Our Tower of London," ordering him to "deliver the body of Adolph Thion," awaiting "trial and delivery" on the charge of "an act of espionage," the reason for the removal (inscribed in a clerkly hand) being "for trial within the jurisdiction of our Lord Lieutenant-General of Ireland."

Every space was filled save one. The date below one of the signatures.

"That's sure a dandy piece of work," said Benson.

"It looks good from here," said a voice, and Benson swung round with an oath.

"No noise—quietly—no bad language. I was raised in a Christian home, Benson."

"Put your little gun down, Colonel," said the forger; "I ain't no hog for battle."

"Good man, but whisper; stand over there and let me see the work of art."

Haynes bent over the table and read.

"Fine! Everything except the date. Fill that in too."

Benson stared.

"Fill it in. I'm going to get you out of all your trouble. I hate to see an old lag in bad. My, Frank, I never thought you'd come down to helping the enemies of Uncle Sam."

Benson grinned uncomfortably.

"I guess it didn't strike me that way, chief," he said virtuously. "If I'd thought—"

"I know, you'd have preferred death to dishonour. Get along with that date."

The man sat at the table and wrote with that stiff, jerky action which is characteristic of all the best forgers, whilst Haynes sorted the blanks and extracted two.

"Now fill in these. The same stamp—I see you have the Home Office seal—and the same signature will do. Address it to The Master of the Sailing Ship Palagonia. That's right. Now in the other space write. 'From London Docks to Tristan d'Acuna.' Done that? Excellent! Now write 'Close custody' in that space, and in the other fill in the name of Adolph Thion. You can fill in his personal description, you know it by heart."

For ten minutes the forger worked, and finally the document was complete with signature, seal, and counter-signature.

When it was finished Haynes folded all the papers and put them in his pocket.

"That is your hat and coat, I think? Put 'em on, it's raining, I believe, though I haven't been out of the house since nine—"

"Oh! you were in all the time?" commented Mr Benson without surprise. "Slammed the door and hid in the hall. I once did a job that way."

"Very elementary," apologised Haynes. "Now, pocket your wad, for you're not coming back here again."

"The wad is pocketed—you can betcher life," said Benson, with a certain satisfaction. "What are you going to do with me?"

"Put you under observation for the night and hand you one of those deportation forms you so obligingly filled—only it will be a real one."

"I'll take your word there's to be no jailing," said Benson.

"Not unless you're wanted on another charge. Go first down the stairs, and don't talk."

They crept down the carpeted stairway, past the big saloon, from whence came a murmur of voices, and out into the stormy street.

As to what happened that night, we have only the bald official narrative supplied to the departments concerned. From this it seems that at three o'clock in the morning two detectives went to the Palace Tower Prison, delivered their papers, which were in proper order, and carried away with them a tall and querulous German.

What happened after that nobody knows. The Palagonia sailed on the ebb tide, and the river police heard voices raised in altercation, and a reference to "another one," but gathered that some of the crew had come aboard in the darkness in a condition which is erroneously described by total abstainers as "merry." At any rate, the Palagonia sailed away, and may or may not have reached Tristan d'Acuna. It is a very long voyage, and there is no cable to the island. It would not fail to be an unpleasant journey for any but a hardened seaman, and "Adolph Thion" did not fill this description—the missing Hohenzollern was anything but a seafaring man.

In course of time the mystery of the missing prisoner came to Haynes for solution.

"I'd rather not touch the case, sir," he said. "I fear there has been some illegality in the matter which may reflect discredit on a Government department."

His chief looked at him. searchingly, but Haynes did not so much as bat a lid.

CHAPTER III

SUNK WITHOUT TRACE

On the morning of April 17 two men were arrested in Cable Street, in the East End of London, on a charge of stealing from a marine store dealer, or, as they call it, a "rag shop," property valued at fourteen shillings. The theft was one of those commonplace happenings which in these days of restricted paper supply would stand a very good chance of not being mentioned.

Only one newspaper, the Evening Herald, of London, thought the circumstances merited mention.

Yet scarcely had two lines been written by a sub in need of an item to fill a column than every newspaper in London received from the Counter Espionage Bureau:—

"The press is requested to publish no account of the proceedings at Millwall Police Court against two men—Higgs and Brinkley—charged with larceny, or to the intervention of the military authorities."

Whereupon some hundred or so sub-editors turned up the report of the proceedings, and asked their puzzled confrères what there was in the attempted theft of an old leather portfolio valued at 14 shillings to merit Government interference.

The circumstances revealed in the verbatim report of the case were these:—

At ten o'clock on the morning in question two men, who afterwards gave their names as Henry Higgs and Thomas Brinkley, entered the marine store of Morris Lipski and asked him if he had any old ships' instruments for sale. Lipski replied that he never kept such things by him, as there was a ready sale to a certain Government Department of all scientific apparatus, even old parts of such, whatever might be their condition.

The two men, who had the appearance of being common sailors, and were roughly and poorly dressed, then asked if Lipski had any old clothing suitable for tropical wear. Lipski, it appears, had two such suits made of silk twill which had come into his possession a few weeks before. The men examined these, and though they were old and shabby paid the price which the dealer demanded. They asked where Lipski had purchased these, and he replied that they formed part of a lot, including a number of books and a shabby leather portfolio, which he had purchased from a tailor.

Higgs then said and Brinkley asked to see the portfolio. The books consisted of three volumes. Two were scientific works on chemistry, one in French and the other in German; one was a Spanish grammar. Those the men purchased, again making no objection to the price which the junk man set or attempting to haggle. Over the question of the writing case, however, a difficulty arose. Lipski had sold this—a fact he had forgotten for the moment when he offered it to the men—to his brother-in-law, but it had not been delivered. All at once Lipski's memory reminded him of the transaction, and he refused to sell.

When their offer for the old portfolio rose first to £5 and then to £10 Lipski was at first astonished and then suspicious. He refused to part with the case at any price, and the more eager they were to buy the more obstinate was he in refusing.

Presently the men left the shop and immediately afterwards Lipski missed from the shelf where he had placed it the portfolio, which was no more than a big envelope of limp leather which could be rolled up and easily concealed (as in fact it was concealed) in a man's pocket. He immediately gave chase, and overtook the two men just as they were getting into a taxi-cab at the end of the street in which his shop was situated.

Fortunately there was a policemen handy, and the men were arrested and convoyed to Lemon Street Police Station. They were brought up and remanded, and a week later came up for judgment.

That was the story of the crime. The Police Court proceedings were tame and conventional until the moment when the Magistrate was about to deal summarily with the case on one of the prisoners' assurance that the portfolio had been taken absent-mindedly and that there was neither need nor reason for theft—a plea supported by the fact that both men had plenty of money.

At this point, when the Magistrate was preparing to deliver a homily on the suspicious carelessness of the prisoners and discharge them, an officer had pushed his way into Court, handed his card to the Magistrate, and had requested a further remand. This the Magistrate had granted, and there the matter ended so far as the Police Court reporter was concerned, though he permitted himself the vague and cautious opinion that "further developments were pending."

The officer whose surprising arrival had made so great a difference to the fate of the larcenists was Major Haynes.

In the Magistrate's private room he explained.

"I'm sorry to give you such short notice, sir," he said, "but it was only an hour ago that I secured the information which induced me to act."

"It seems a fairly ordinary type of larceny—if it was larceny, and not, as there was a possibility, a genuine mistake on the part of the men," said the Magistrate. "I presume you want them held for inquiries?"

Haynes nodded. "That and other things." he said.

"They are English, I think?" said the official.

"Neither is English—though they speak English perfectly. By the shape of 'Brinkley's' head I should say he was Scandinavian. They are both members of the crew of a Scandinavian vessel at present in London Dock."

Haynes interviewed the prosecutor and the prisoners, took charge of the portfolio, and stopping only to dispatch a telegram, he drove back to his office a little puzzled by his own discoveries. It was by the merest luck that he had read a week-old account of the "crime," had connected it with an odd scrap of information which had come to him some time before and had taken precipitate action.

Arrived at the office he went straight to his chief and informed him of what he had done.

"What I am going to do next," he confessed, "the writing case will decide. If that does not solve the mystery, nothing will."

He laid on the desk the black leather portfolio and General Marriness took it up and examined it.

"Made abroad—in a Latin country," he said, "probably Spain."

"Or South America."

"Or South America. Initials printed on in gold, but the gold has worn off: 'K.S.', and underneath: 'Lab. K.W.'"

He doubled it up.

"There's a paper of some kind between the layers of leather," he said, and Haynes nodded.

"Sewn in—I've been trying to find the entrance of a pocket," he said, "if you look at the stitches with a magnifying glass you will see they are comparatively new and sewn by an amateur. As I say, the contents of that paper should explain the inexplicable."

He seated himself at the other side of the desk, took out his penknife and picked the stitches. Presently a corner of the thin leather envelope was flapping down. He put in his hand and brought it out holding between his fingers a creased sheet of thin paper which contained a few lines of writing.

Haynes whistled. "In German," he said, and taking pencil and paper, wrote.

When he had finished he leaned back in his chair and laughed.

"That's a joke on me," he chuckled and read—

"Ah, clever Englishman! You thought you had discovered a great secret! Learn that we Germans can match cunning with cunning and the formula is safely hidden.—'The Wizard.'"

The two men looked at one another.

"Well, what do you know about that?" asked Haynes admiringly, "and what the dickens is 'the formula' and who is 'The Wizard?'"

"A pretty problem," said the general, "now tell me Haynes, what made you go down to the court and hold these men?"

Haynes thought a moment.

"I am marshaling events in their order," he said. "The whole case is new to me. In the first place, I remember getting a report about three weeks ago that Veille—a German agent who is now under arrest—had been visiting junk shops making inquiries for a black box. Then I heard that another man, also under suspicion, had made the rounds of East End rag shops inquiring for tortoise-rimmed spectacles and scientific books in German. In fact, this man Lipski with whom I had a talk to-day, remembered that such inquiries had been made, and because he had either forgotten such things, or that he did not know at the time he had them, he told the inquirer that he had nothing of the sort in stock. Now I ask you, why is Germany employing agents to make the round of London junk shops, and why particularly is the search confined to the East End of London?"

There was a knock at door and a commissionaire came in.

"Inspector Cowley, sir," he said addressing Haynes.

"Good—has he anybody with him?"

"Yes sir—a seafaring man."

"Good again—can I see them here sir?" he asked the General, "I wired Cowley to bring this man by taxi. Show them in here, sergeant."

A minute later the visitors came in. Inspector Cowley, a grey-haired police official, and with him a tall, bearded man, with an amiable grin for Haynes and a friendly nod for the General.

"Sit down, Mr Parson," said Haynes. "I want to ask you a few questions—do you know this?" He held up the leather portfolio.

"Yes, sir."

"You sold that and several other articles to Lipski, of Cable Street?"

"Quite right, sir—honestly come by."

"You also sold other articles to various marine store dealers?"

"Right you are—honestly come by."

"I'm not doubting your honesty," smiled Haynes, "but perhaps you will tell me the circumstances under which these things came into your possession."

The man put his big hands on his knees and cleared his throat. Apparently it was a story he had told before, for he started off with a run.

"Out of Valparaiso with a cargo of nitrates we was—"

"What ship?" interrupted Haynes, pencil in hand.

"Oregon City, Port of Glasgow, 4750 tons, M'Fee Brothers owners; captain's name George Barton."

"Go on," nodded Haynes.

"Accordin' to some we had no Admiralty sailin' orders. Accordin' to others we did—you know how sailors yarn? Well, anyway, a hundred an' fifty miles west of Madeira, at four bells in the middle watch, up pops a submarine, and—biff. No warnin'—no nothin'—biff! The Oregon City went down by the head in five minutes. Me an' a friend of mine got a boat away, and us two, the second officer, the cook, and an apprentice got clear of the ship. We didn't see the submarine. He went off after another ship. We pulled about lookin' for survivors, but there wasn't any, an' after hangin' round for an hour we slipped the sail an' made a course for Madeira. That night, or rather at daybreak next morning, we come upon a raft."

This was evidently the climax of his tale, for he paused and looked around.

"The only thing on that raft was a little old man an' a big black box. When we come up to it he was sittin' with his back to the box, an' was as near dead as makes no difference. We pulled alongside, though we hadn't got too much water and no food worth speakin' about, and I slipped on to the raft. He opened his eyes, the old man did, an' said somethin' in German. Not understanding German, I made no reply. And then he died an' we committed him to the deep," the sonorous phrase pleased him, and he repeated, "we committed his body into the deep. I took the box, hopin' for miracles. There was no money in the old man's pocket; an' nothin' in the box except a lot of books, that case, a few old suits of clothes, a couple of medicine bottles, some undershirts, and such like. We was picked up by a Funchal trawler that afternoon, and that's the story, gentlemen."

"You brought the box to England ?" asked Haynes.

"'Naturally—as a curio. I got hard up and sold it. A lady I live with did most of the sellin'—trust a woman to take the last rags a feller's got," he added bitterly.

"You are sure that there was nothing besides these things, clothes, books, etcetera?"

The man hesitated.

"Well sir, without the word of a lie, there was. This old gentleman had a gold ring. Like a wedding ring it was, but the inside was covered with fine writing—you'd want a microscope to read it."

"What did you do with that?" asked Haynes quickly.

"Popped it—here's the ticket."

He plunged into his trousers pocket and produced a miscellaneous collection of string, plug tobacco, dirty scraps of paper. From this he extracted a grimy pawn ticket.

"Pledged with Harrisons, of Wharf Street," said Haynes.

"That's right sir," said the man. "I can tell you I'm glad to have this matter officially investigated. I'm fed up with the inquiries I've had about that box. All sorts of chaps have been to see me."

"That I am beginning to understand," said Haynes. "Have you told anybody about the ring?"

Again the man hesitated.

"Not till this morning, sir. A very affable gentleman called to see me, and I don't mind telling you that he behaved handsomely—and I can do with it I'm sailing next week in the—"

"You told him about the ring?" interrupted Haynes.

"I did, sir."

"Did he ask to see it?"

"He did," remarked Mr Parson complacently. "He wanted to buy the ticket, and I'd have sold it to him, only my old woman had it and she happened to be out. She only came back just before this gentleman arrived," he nodded to Cowley.

"You have no idea as to who this old man was on the raft?"

"No, sir, except his name, Karl Sieglemann—Professor Karl Sieglemann."

"Professor Karl Sieglemann," repeated Haynes. "How did you know that?" he asked sharply.

"Written on his underclothes, sir."

"K.S.," said the General across the table. "You will find the German 'Who's Who' up there."

Haynes walked to the shelf, and taking down the bulky volume, laid it on the table and rapidly turned the leaves.

"Here you are, 'Karl Sieglemann, professor of chemistry,'" he read, "'director until 1903 of the Kaiser Wilhelm Laboratory, Dresden'—that's the fellow—'Lab. K.W.', sir. 'Now resident in Mexico City and employed by Mexican Government.'"

Haynes read the paragraph again and shut the book, and for a minute was deep in thought.

"That will do for the moment, Parson," he said; "I may want you again."

When the inspector and his charge had departed the General asked—

"What do you make of it, Haynes?"

"I am trying to remember. I know the name so well, and it is associated in my mind with explosives."

He went back to his office and sent the patient Dane in search of records. An hour later he returned to his chief's bureau.

"I've got it," he said triumphantly. "Look here"—he laid a little sheaf of press cuttings on the desk—"do you remember some time ago a cable coming to this country that a German professor had discovered a new explosive? The American Government intercepted a wireless message from Berlin calling the old man home."

"I remember now," said the General.

"Do you remember there was also a reference to Sieglemann in the letters which were taken from the German agent, Archibald, at Falmouth? Here is the reference. The letters were published in the American press, and a selection were also published on this side. What I am reading to you now is a portion of a letter which was sent from the Austrian Ambassador in Washington to the Foreign Minister in Vienna.

"I regret I can give you no better news about Professor Sieglemann. Our experts are satisfied that his new explosive is a valuable discovery, and would considerably assist our cause, but the old man refuses to commit the formula to paper, and we are endeavouring to arrange a passage for him to Scandinavia. He insists upon carrying it to Germany himself, and nothing we can do can dissuade him."

Haynes finished reading and looked up.

"That's the elucidation of our mystery," he said. "Sieglemann sailed probably incognito. His ship was sunk by a German submarine, the commander of which was, of course, ignorant of the precious freight the vessel was carrying—it was probably the ship that the U-boat went off to sink after torpedoing the Oregon City. This seaman lands the box, brings it to Britain, the German Intelligence get to know of the circumstances, probably through the Professor's underclothes being offered for sale in London, and send their agents to buy up from the various junk shops every bit of stuff that Parson sold."

"And the formula?" asked the General.

"Obviously the writing on the ring," said Haynes.

He pressed a bell and the commissionaire appeared in the doorway.

"Get a taxi," he said.

He turned to the General.

"I am going down to Wharf Street to get this precious formula."

"You think it is in the ring?"

"I'm pretty certain. The old man expected the ship to be searched, and probably planted all sorts of red herrings, including that which we found in the portfolio. The real composition of the explosive is engraved on the inside of his ring. Our job is to get to that pawnshop before the affable gentleman," he said grimly, but as it fell out this part of his plan went astray.

As his taxi-cab turned into Wharf Street it almost collided with a car which turned out into the Commercial Road at full speed.

Haynes saw people running after it, realised that something was wrong, and stopped the cab. A breathless woman gasped the news—

"A man has been shot, sir—somebody's robbed the pawnbroker."

Haynes did not go any further. He saw the crowd around a shop door, glimpsed the policeman's helmet above the heads of the mob, and took his decision. He had no doubt what had been the object of the crime. The ring had gone, and with it a precious secret which would bring death to thousands of his fellow-countrymen—which might indeed make all the difference between victory and defeat.

"You saw that car that nearly collided with us," he said to the driver. "Turn into the main road and follow the direction it went. You can open out and go as fast as you like. I will see that you are not prosecuted. Stop at the first police station."

"That will be Lemon Street, air," said the man.

"That will do excellently," said Haynes, and jumped into the cab.

Ten minutes later the wires that led to the East Coast were humming with the description of a long grey car and Haynes was moving as fast as a London taxicab could carry him eastward.

The car had been seen in Canning Town. It had passed through East Ham, and when the taxi arrived at a little town halfway to Chelmsford Haynes exchanged the taxi for a powerful Daimler and the company of the taxi-driver for three intelligence officers, who had been summoned by 'phone to meet him.

There he learnt the details of the robbery. A smart-looking man had called at the pawnbroker's, had produced a detective's card, and had asked to see the ring, giving the date on which it had been pledged (he had evidently got that from parson). The pawnbroker had produced the ring, and when the man had attempted to leave the shop with it tried to prevent him. There had been a struggle: a shot was fired, which fortunately had done little more than alarm the worthy moneylender.

All that afternoon until it was dark the search continued. Every car that passed through the Eastern Counties was held up and examined. At two o'clock that morning light squadrons of the German fleet stole out of the mist and opened a heavy bombardment upon a certain East Coast town, under cover of which a small motor launch stood inshore and picked up a solitary passenger from a deserted beach.

The coastguard witnessed the incident, and opened fire upon the little boat, but apparently without doing any damage.

Haynes, who was in the bombarded coast town, heard the news, and understood its significance. The attack on the coast was a blind to distract the attention of the guards and to draw in the war vessels which were patrolling the seas in the vicinity of embarkation.

"We shall get nothing by following the German cruisers," said Haynes to the senior naval officer. "You may be sure that by this time our man is on his way to the Belgian coast in his motor boat."

"I'll let you have a destroyer to make a search," said the Commodore.

At dawn Haynes, standing on the rocking bridge of a fast destroyer scout, picked up the motor boat dead ahead. It was moving at racing speed and was within reach of the protecting German minefields when the first gun of the scout crashed forth.

Through his glasses Haynes saw one solitary figure in the stern, waving a mocking salute to his pursuer. Only a glimpse he had, then suddenly something struck the motor launch, a grey column of water speckled with little black objects leapt into the air, and when it had subsided the motor launch was nowhere to be seen.

When the scout came up to the place only one survivor remained. He was a man in civilian attire, who was clinging desperately to a lifebelt, and Haynes' heart leapt as he realised that his surmise had been correct. The scout lowered a boat, and Major Haynes was the first to step into it. They were less than a dozen yards from the shipwrecked man when Haynes saw him take something from his finger and hold it above his head—something round and golden that glittered in the light of the morning sun.

"Spurlos versenkt—sunk without trace," he cried, and dropped the ring into the water, and "sunk without trace" indeed was that remarkable formula which might well have given Germany dominion over the world.

Haynes leant down, and gripping the man by the collar hauled him on board.

"I am a German officer, and I claim the protection which my rank gives me," he said. "You have had all your trouble for nothing," he added triumphantly.

"You haven't exactly had the time of your life," retorted Haynes.

CHAPTER IV

THE GERMAN IRON BOOK

The first time Major Haynes spoke to Elsa Tomass was in the corridor of the Guildhall. To be exact, she spoke to him, a somewhat embarrassing circumstance.

For three days he had sat through the Court-Martial which had been held behind closed doors, listening to the evidence against O'Callaghan Tomass and his pretty wife. Pretty she was indeed, with her round baby face, her golden mop of hair, her violet eyes, and rosebud lips, and there were many in that Court who pitied this flower-like child-wife, and hoped she would escape conviction.

Haynes was not one of these.

On the contrary, throughout those anxious days he had prayed for a miracle of evidence which would enable him to draw the net as tightly about the girl as he had drawn it about her husband. For O'Callaghan Tomass was doomed from the moment when he stepped between his armed guards and faced his judges.

The evidence was clear. Every link held. Not only had he been guilty of espionage and transmitting information by means of a secret wireless plant—he was a brilliant young engineer—but he had materially assisted in the destruction of shipping, and had been caught red-handed in the act of placing a bomb upon an outward-bound cargo boat. Yet the prosecution only touched the fringe of the conspiracy in which Tomass was an agent. Haynes knew there was a bigger thing behind this phase of the conspiracy, and, rightly or wrongly, he associated Elsa Tomass, nee Brandenburg, the daughter of Professor Brandenburg of Dresden University, with this movement.

The circumstances were peculiar. Tomass had met the girl at the Hague, whither he had gone ostensibly to examine an engineering contract in conjunction with the Netherlands Government.

Elsa Brandenburg was admittedly German, admittedly associated with Bureau 6 of the German Foreign Office Intelligence Department, and her arrival in England in the ordinary course of events would have been followed immediately by her arrest and deportation.

When, after a month's acquaintance, she married this young man, she became automatically British, and presented to the British Foreign Office a problem which it hesitated to tackle. There is no law which prevents a German girl from marrying a British subject even though a war is in progress between the two countries, and whatever barriers may be set up against the naturalisation of foreigners are surmounted by the simple processes of matrimony.

Within three months of his arrival in England Tomass was under suspicion. Then followed his arrest.

But though the genius of the counterespionage bureau easily overcame all the difficulties of proving the man's complicity in various political crimes there was no shred of evidence which could convict the girl. The expert men who watched the case called her "The girl who looked ahead." She had guarded herself against every contingency. She brought dozens of unimpeachable witnesses, who proved that she was not connected with any of the acts alleged against her. She had unshakable alibis to establish her presence at places other than where the various crimes were committed, and half-way through the trial she had been discharged, a fact which Haynes had accepted philosophically.

The trial had ended, the prisoner had been removed in custody when he came out of the big Court into the corridor and found himself confronted by the girl. She looked up into his eyes fearlessly, and there was a half-smile upon her lips.

"May I speak to you for a moment, Major Haynes?" she asked.

Haynes bowed courteously, and led her to a room which had been his headquarters in many such trials as this.

"What do you think will happen to my husband?" she asked.

Haynes shrugged his shoulders.

"I am afraid I cannot tell you, Mrs Tomass," he answered. "The Court will promulgate its finding in due course."

"Will you tell me this," she demanded; "do you think there is any chance that he will escape the death penalty?"

Haynes looked at her.

"I do not think there is any chance," he said.

"Thank you," she said quietly. "He was very foolish, very reckless. He would never listen to advice." She spoke half to herself, and Haynes wondered what the trend of that advice had been.

For himself he did not doubt that the advice had been directed to avoiding unnecessary risks which Tomass had undoubtedly taken.

"What are you going to do with me?" she asked.

"Again I am not able to tell you," said Haynes. "I am afraid we may have to deport or intern you."

"But you have proved nothing against me!"

Haynes smiled.

"You want to say something," she said. "Say it. I don't care what it is."

"I only want to say that I do not think you are innocent," he said quietly. "I believe you are even more guilty than your husband. I believe you are certainly one of the most dangerous people in this country, that you planned all these outrages, but, being much more clever than the unfortunate people you employ, you have escaped the consequence of the crimes. Therefore, it is best to deport you."

She bit her lips in thought, and in spite of her composure there was a look of fury in her violet eyes.

"At least you will do nothing until—" she hesitated, and Haynes know that she was referring to her husband's execution.

"I can promise you nothing," he said, rising to end the interview. "The matter is not in my hands, but I do not imagine that the British Government will deal harshly with you."

"Thank you," she said, and rose to go. "One more question. It is rather an indiscreet one I am afraid."

"Then don't ask it," he smiled.

"I must, for my own protection," she looked down.

For some reason it seemed that she did not want to meet his eyes.

"Did—did any of the witnesses speak of the Iron Book?"

"The Iron Book?" said Haynes, puzzled.

"Then they didn't speak of it," she said quickly, looking up at him.

"I've no recollection of any such reference," said Haynes. "Would it be indiscreet on my part to ask what the Iron Book is?"

She raised her eyebrows in astonishment, and laughed softly.

"Oh, please, Major Haynes, do not pretend with me. It is the only thing I ever heard my poor husband speak about openly. That wonderful Iron Book, which was in existence, and which he was so anxious to see—and which I was just as anxious that he should not see."

"Will you sit down again, Mrs Tomass?" said Haynes. "I am interested in this matter. Perhaps you can tell me some more."

She leant back in the chair in an easy attitude.

"In every belligerent country, so the story goes," she began, "there is a copy of the Iron book. It is called an Iron Book because it is bound in steel, and it is in the possession of one trustworthy man who answers with his life for its safe custody. It contains information about all prominent people in that country, but especially about those who have German ancestors or German relatives," she shivered. "It is a book which is never finished," she went on. "New pages come to the holder week by week. That is why I am so anxious to know whether it was mentioned. I am going to be frank with you, Major Haynes," she went on. "I believe my name is in the book. I am 26. I do not look it? Still I am 26. My past has not been a very happy one, and there was one particular incident in my life—I was a girl of eighteen at the time—which I am anxious should never be known, especially to my husband."

She dropped her eyes again, and Haynes was sympathetically silent.

"I have no reason to like you, Major Haynes," she said, looking up. "But I want to ask you one thing, and it is a request that I have no right to make, and perhaps that you have no right to grant."

"Then you may be sure that I shall not grant it," said Haynes.

"I am not so sure that you cannot grant it. I make the appeal to you not as the wife of a political prisoner to an officer of the law, but as a woman to a man. I want you to promise me this, that if the Iron Book ever comes into your possession you will read what is written about me before you hand the book to anybody else. If you think you can destroy my record without injuring your country or committing any flagrant breach of your duty I want you to destroy it. If you think that such an action would be inconsistent with your duty, I shall be content if you allow other eyes to read the story of my wretched life. It is really not much I ask."

Haynes thought a moment.

"I can promise you that I will first examine the record myself, though it is very unlikely that I shall destroy it."

She rose. She did not offer her hand.

"I am grateful to you," she said in a low voice, and without another word she swept from the room.

It was not until two months later that Haynes heard again of the Iron Book. It was on a warm day in June, when soft breezes were blowing through the windows of his little office at Whitehall. He sat at his table, and he was at the moment extremely busy. He was playing patience with every appearance of concentration, but one half of his brain, the business half, was at that moment very far away.

His assistant looked across at him disapprovingly, for Captain Dane was, to say the least, in a condition of exasperation, a condition into which it was Haynes' greatest joy to drive him. For Haynes had been holding forth on the mystery of commonplace things, a favourite topic of his, and Dane, who detested all that savoured of the common, had just read a letter from which he defied his superior to extract romance.

"Read it out again," said Haynes, putting the red six on the black seven with a little "Cluck!" of annoyance as he discovered that he might have taken that step three minutes before.

"'Dear sir,'" began Dane.

"Wait a moment," interrupted Haynes. "The address, I think, is Pauly Lodge, Sydenham Hill Crescent, a highly respectable residential thoroughfare, with £120-a-year houses mostly tenanted by retired tradesmen."

"I don't know the street," said Dane, "but I will take your word."

"'Dear Sir,—I think it is only right that you should know that in this neighbourhood there is a very dangerous gang of German spies. Surely these people ought not to be allowed at large. During the last raid I myself distinctly saw signal lamps flash from a field at the back of my house—which stands upon a rise—and I have reported the matter to the local police authorities, without, however, getting anything done. I have reason to believe also that a certain Mr Grunert, who occupies a villa near mine, has mysterious visitors. Verb sap. I enclose my card, and am, &c., &c.—Lionel Poggitt.'"

"Well, can you extract any tragedy front that except the tragedy of the spy maniac, who is quite certain he is surrounded by deadly enemies?"

"And very likely he is," said Haynes,

He threw his cards into confusion, gathered the pack neatly and stacked them into the drawer. Then he looked at his watch.

"Whether there is drama, comedy, tragedy, or whether it is a very uninteresting and commonplace story we shall learn," he said, looking at his watch, "for Mr Poggitt has threatened to call, and is due in exactly one minute, my dear Watson."

"Watson? Who the dickens do you mean?" asked the startled Dane. "And why is Poggitt calling?"

Haynes chuckled.

"As to the first part of your question, I see you are unacquainted with a detective classic, otherwise, you would not only recognise the name but also a situation which occurs and recurs in the biography of a famous criminologist. As to the second part, Mr Poggitt comes because I have telegraphed to him."

There was a knock at the door.

"Come in," said Haynes. "This, I think, is the announcement of our visitor."

In this surmise he proved to be wholly inaccurate. The visitor was a very junior officer in search of a "minute."

"Which shows bad stage management, my dear Watson," said Haynes.

"For heaven's sake don't call me Watson!" snarled Dane.

It was an hour later when the commissionaire ushered in a tall thin man, dressed severely in the frock coat and top hat which is inseparable from a certain type of commercial prosperity.

"Sit down, Mr Poggitt," said Haynes "This is my assistant, Captain Dane. Yon are almost punctual."

The visitor looked at him dubiously.

"Ah, yes," he said, not knowing whether to be amused or to offer the tribute of a smile. "I had your telegram this morning, Major Haynes, and I am very much obliged to you for this opportunity." He opened a small leather bag he carried and took out a letter.

"This is the communication I referred to in my telegram," he said a little pompously.

Haynes took the envelope and glanced at the date-mark. Then, he took out a sheet of notepaper. There was no name or address, only a dozen lines written in a stiff and angular hand:—

"Understand you have informed the authorities about Grunert. This man is very dangerous, and is in possession of the Iron Book, containing names of prominent citizens who will be held to ransom if German Army arrives in England. Your name is there, also names of German agents in this country."

It was signed "A Friend."

"Iron Book!" repeated Haynes. "H'm!" He handed the letter to his assistant. "What do you make of that?" he asked. Dane read it through.

"Probably a hoax," he said. "How did they come to know, that you had sent the letter to us?"

"That's the mystery," said Mr Poggitt in a tone of melancholy triumph. "Nobody knew—"

"Except, of course, your wife," interrupted Haynes, "and probably your married daughter and possibly your butler, and as likely as not most of the servants in your house."

Mr Poggitt looked nonplussed.

"I certainly mentioned it to my wife," he admitted, "and I can swear to the honesty of Thomas."

"That is your butler, Thomas Thomson, age 56, eminently respectable, member of the Wesleyan Methodist Church, born in Greenwich, &c., &c., &c. Go on, Mr Poggitt, you interest me."

Mr Poggitt looked from one to the other. "Well, that is all," he said. "What do you think of it?"

"Tell me one thing before I answer you," said Haynes, leaning back in his chair, "how is it you came to write to me about this letter? The fact that I am the chief of the Counter-Espionage Bureau, is not exactly advertised in the daily press. Who suggested my name?"

"I am glad you asked that," said Mr Poggitt, brightening up as he remembered there was still a sensation in store. "As you know, I have been suspicious for some time about this man Grunert, and have had him kept under observation. It must have become known that I was acting as a sort of—er—"

"Intelligence officer," suggested Haynes.

"Exactly," said Mr Poggitt, "as an intelligence officer. This is not the first letter I have received." He pointed to the epistle on the desk. "A week ago I had a telegram saying, 'Consult Major Haynes, Room 2006, the War Office.' I thought at first it was from an old friend of mine, Meyers (of Meyers, Mean & Willcox), to whom I had confided my suspicions, but Mr Meyers knew nothing of the matter. Unfortunately I did not keep the telegram, but I remember it was handed in at Ludgate Hill Post Office."

"I see," said Haynes. He was silent for a moment, and then—"All you tell me is very interesting: Can you give me any information about Grunert?"

"He seems a respectable man," confessed Mr Poggitt reluctantly. "So far as I know he pays his way, but does not have much to do with his neighbours. Indeed, we know very little about him, although he has lived in the neighbourhood for eight years."

"Any family?" asked Haynes.

"None. He had one man-servant and one maid-servant—an ex-member of the Metropolitan Police Force and his wife. The man has joined up as an instructor, and the wife carries on."

Haynes scratched his chin.

"Is that all you can tell me?"

"I am afraid it is," said Mr Poggitt in a tone of disappointment.

"I will investigate this matter," said Haynes conventionally, and rose to shake hands with his visitor. When he had gone he turned to Dane.

"Well, there's romance for you. We shall find Mr Grunert in possession of the Iron Book."

Dane looked at him helplessly.

"Then I presume," he said with heavy sarcasm, "you will do the obvious thing—raid the house, seize this precious Iron Book—"

"This is hardly the moment for the obvious," replied Haynes, in so serious a tone that Dane looked up in surprise. "It is not expected of me either that I shall follow on conventional lines."

"Expected?" Dane was puzzled, "by Mr Poggitt?"

Major Haynes laughed, but made no reply. Nevertheless, that night three plain clothes officers called at Pauly Lodge armed with a search warrant, and, Mr Grunert protesting, they searched the house from attic to cellar and discovered nothing.

At eleven o'clock the police officers departed, leaving a very injured neutral gentleman on the door step. At twelve o'clock a dark figure stole from the back garden of the house, passed through a little wicket gate, and walked rapidly in the direction of Lordship Lane. The man carried under his arm a small flat parcel. Once or twice he looked round as though he thought he was being followed. But if there was a shadow behind him it would have been well-described.

The man reached the railway arch which crosses Lordship Lane at the point where the station of that name is situate, and stopped. He looked to the left and right, saw nobody in sight, and began slowly to retrace his steps the way he had come. He had reached the corner of Sydenham Hill Crescent when his arm was gripped, and he swung round.

"Let me relieve you of that little packet," said Major Haynes.

He pulled the parcel away, and the man made no resistance. Haynes whistled softly, and from behind the low wall of a neighbouring front garden two men rose and came silently toward them.

"Take this man into custody," said Haynes. "How far did you go, by the way?" he asked his prisoner.

"What's that to do with you?" said the prisoner sullenly.

"I am only curious to know," said Haynes. "I didn't follow you, for I knew you were coming back."

"You can't do anything to me," said the man. "I was told to take this book down to Lordship Lane, and if the gentleman wasn't there I was to give it to I was to bring it back."

"I believe you," said Haynes. "Do you live in the neighbourhood?"

The prisoner admitted that he was a greengrocer's assistant, and that he did odd jobs for Mr Grunert. He had called that night at Mr Grunert's villa by arrangement.

"I believe your story is true," said Haynes again, "and to-morrow you will probably be released. In the meantime, Jackson," he turned to the second man, "I think you had better pull in Mr Grunert," he said, "if he has not already departed. I think the odds are against your catching him by the way."

He proved to be correct, Mr Grunert being conspicuous by his absence when the police paid a return visit to his villa.

It was half-past twelve when Haynes' car drew up in front of the little side door which gave access to his office. The pavement was not deserted. The commissionaire who stood before the door was talking to a lady, and even before he had stepped from the car Haynes recognised the visitor.

"Beg pardon, sir," said the commissionaire. "this lady wants to see you."

"This is an unexpected pleasure, Mrs Tomass," said Haynes.

"Can I speak to you for five minutes?" said the girl.

He looked at her, the old smile, which she hated, in his eyes.

"You would like to talk to me in the street, I presume?"

"I should prefer that," she said hurriedly. "You have the book."

"How did you know?" he asked.

She hesitated

"I learn things," she said. "There are still many misguided friends of my husband who persist in believing that I share his secrets. You remember your promise?"

"I have not forgotten it," he said gravely.

"You will not let anybody see my record until you have read it?" she asked.

He nodded.

"Thank you a thousand times."

This time she offered her hand, and he was surprised at the strength in her grip. He watched her as she walked to the end of the side street and turned into Whitehall. He saw her joined by two men, who stopped and spoke to her, and then the three disappeared round the corner. Carrying the book under his arm, he went up the stairs to his room, threw open the windows, and locked the door.

Then he opened the parcel. It was of brown paper, tied about with brown tape, and within the wrapping was a flat steel box fashioned like a book and fastened with a clasp lock, the key for which hung suspended by a bit of string from the box.

He held it in his hand, and found it remarkably light. The steel, he could tell, was thin and well tempered. He put the key in the lock, but before turning it he opened a cupboard and extracted and fitted something which he had found very useful in the days of his active service.

Then he returned to the table and snapped round the key. The pressure inside must have been a terrific one. The lid flew open with such force that, striking and rebounding on the table, it was bent half-double, and in the shock of the release the box leapt from his hand and fell on the floor. There was no explosion. Only in two seconds the whole room was filled with a thin fog-like mist, the mist in which chlorine poison gas dissolves in the process of vaporisation. There was sufficient gas in the room to kill a platoon of men.

"Very interesting," said Haynes aloud, and his voice was strangely muffled and hollow, for his face was hidden behind the gas mask he had fitted before he turned the key.

"Is this sufficiently romantic for you?" he asked the next morning, and Dane admitted that it was.

"She planned this the day her husband was sentenced. She invented the Iron Book on the spur of the moment—don't forget she is 'The Girl Who Looks Ahead.' I was waiting for two months for some new reference to the Iron Book to crop up, and at last it came. She wanted me to have the medicine all alone. That is why she told me the sad story of her sinful past.

"I was not quite sure what form her grand surprise was going to take. For a long time I suspected a bomb, but I rejected that idea, because she gave me credit for sufficient intelligence to know that I would not be taken in by an infernal machine. It is so easily detected. It weighs too much, and makes an infernal row. Grunert was the agent selected to put the Iron Book into my possession. All these stories of Grunert being a German spy were designed to tickle my curiosity. I knew the book could not be found in his house. You see, that girl looked ahead. She knew that I would not be content with a police search, and that I should be looking for somebody who was removing the book by stealth."

"But how do you account for the fact?" asked Dane, "that you hit upon the very night when this man was carrying the book away from the house?"

Haynes laughed.

"My dear chap," he said, "that unfortunate greengrocer had been carrying the book every night for a week. I myself had seen him twice. Every night for a week Mrs Tomass had been waiting to intercept me at the War Office to remind me of my promise, and every night for a week I had had two of my men waiting to arrest that enterprising lady as soon as I gave the signal that she had had her final interview. I don't think she will escape so easily this time," he added thoughtfully.

CHAPTER V

UNMASKING A PEACE PLOT

Again and again we have heard of the almost unbelievable cleverness of diplomatic spies, but their stupidity is not often recorded with such dramatic terseness as in this little tale.

Major Haynes was descending the steps of his club when a well-dressed man slipped and stumbled, and would have fallen but for the fact that he flung his arms wildly about the body of the major.

"Steady, the Buffs!" said Haynes.

"I'm very sorry, sir," gasped the other; "piece of orange peel or something—much obliged, I'm sure."

Haynes looked at him, taking in the man, from his obviously new silk hat to his obviously new patent shoes.

"Can the bird of paradise speak with the voice of the crow?" he asked wonderingly, "in other words, can the man about town in all his giddy splendor, speak in the language of Houndsditch?"

"What do you mean, my good man?" demanded the immaculate stumbler haughtily. "What are you holding my arm for?"

"For better or for worse," murmured Haynes, and jerked his head to a man who was loitering outside the club. "Take this fellow, Drake—his name is Tony Birdweed, and he is a notorious pickpocket. He has just relieved me of a pocketbook which you will probably discover up his sleeve. Is it a cop, Tony?"

"It's a cop, guv'nor," admitted the well-dressed prisoner with some bitterness.

Haynes followed his captive, and interviewed him in a cell at Cannon Row, for he was very anxious to know who were the parties employing Tony to secure his pocketbook.

"I'll tell you the truth without the word of a lie," said the prisoner, much more comfortable sitting in his shirt sleeves and with his high, collar removed. "A little Yid named Metchiffski put me on to the job. I only came out of 'stir' last week—three months I got for larceny—and he met me at the prison an' put the job up to me. I don't want to give him away, but if it's a national matter, sir, why I'm goin' to spill it. I hate all Germans, an' if I had my way about the Kaiser—"

"I know—you'd pinch his watch—but that's beside the point. Did Metchiffski tell you why he wanted my pocket-book?"

"Yes sir. He said you'd got a note for a thousand rubles that his brother had forged an' if I got it there'd be no evidence against him. He said he didn't care what happened to him so long as his brother was saved."

"How touching," said the unsympathetic Haynes; "and he didn't care what happened to you either?"

"Looks like it," said Mr Birdweed gloomily; "I was a proper can to try it on you. I deserve all I get major, but make it as light as you can for me."

A 'phone message called the inspector of Commercial Road station.

"Arrest and detain Abraham Metchiffski, 776 Sydney Rents," Haynes instructed, and he heard an exclamation of surprise from the other end of the wire.

"That's a curious coincidence," came the reply. "We've just had a report in that this man shot himself five minutes ago!"

Haynes hung up the receiver with a frown. He was still frowning when he strode into his office and plumped down at his desk.

Dane looked up from his interminable filing. "What's up?" he asked.

Haynes narrated the events of the previous half-hour.

"What was it all about?" he asked irritably. "There is absolutely nothing of value in my pocket-book—that is to say, nothing of value to anybody but myself—and yet Metchiffski engages a man to rob me, sets another man to watch Birdweed, and when the pickpocket is arrested and his employer is notified—I presume by telephone—Metchiffski shoots himself!"

He took out his pocketbook and laid it on the table. Dane picked it up, and examined it interestedly. It was of polished crocodile skin, with silver corner pieces and a silver monogram at one corner.

"Turn it out," said Haynes, "perhaps you can find an explanation. I confess that I cannot."

"A warrant card," recited Dane as he extracted the articles one by one, "two tailors' bills receipted (strangely enough), an all-stations season ticket, a newspaper cutting about submarines losses—he could have cut that out of the Times himself—a piece of sticking plaster, and your credentials so far as I can see—diplomatic passport and the usual junk."

"We must assume," said Haynes, "that Metchiffski went to a great deal of trouble and expense to secure something which he could not get in any other way. We must also assume that when he hired a pickpocket to rob me he did not contemplate suicide in case that thief failed or was captured—a shrewd person, as I conceive this man to be, would not put his life in the hands of common thief. Therefore, we must assume that his death was not directly due to the arrest of Birdweed, but that some other cause must be found for what the coroner will describe as a rash act."

"It's rum," admitted Dane.

"I have asked Drake to go east and report," said Haynes. "When he returns we shall be able to judge better how rum it is."

Drake's report, when it came, threw a new light on the subject. The Russian was a master tailor, who employed some twenty workpeople. He was a man unknown to the police in the more sinister sense. He occupied three rooms in a block of buildings known as Sydney Rents, one of which served him as an office. In this office he had been found dead. A telephone receiver was in one hand, a revolver in the other.

People on the floor above had heard two shots, as they thought, and, rushing down, had discovered the man sprawling over his desk.

"I made an inspection of the room," said Officer Drake, "and examined the body. He was shot, as far as I can judge, by somebody standing in the doorway."

"Murdered?"

The officer nodded.

"They heard two shots. The first was one fired by Metchiffski. The bullet went through the wall six inches from the place where a man would be standing, supposing he was at the door and had just opened it. The second was fired by the murderer, who used a Browning. Metchiffski's gun was a Smith-Wesson hammerless. I read the case this way: The Russian was taking a message from the 'phone when the door opened. He was evidently expecting a visitor, for his revolver must have been on the desk or very handy. He looked up and shot straight away. The door could only have been half open from the position of the mark on the wall."

"Was anything found?" asked Haynes.

"This."

"This" was an exercise book of a fairly common type. Haynes turned the cover and raised his eyebrows. Four photographs were neatly pasted on the first page, and they were photographs of himself! He turned the leaf. Four more photographs of himself and so through the book, except on the last page. They were enlargements of shots evidently taken by one skilled in photography, and showed only his head. They were photographs of Haynes smiling, pictures of him side-faced, full-faced, even views of the back of his head. Beneath each was written a word or two in Russian. Under one was "Difficult—avoid." Under another "Safe." Under a third "Very good—safe."

The last page of the book had no pictures, but instead were written scores of meaningless sentences, These were in English:—

"Patronizing and witty." A few American phrases such as "Go to it," "Sure," and Beat it" were among these. "Sorry to inconvenience you," was another. This and other pages had evidently been well handled, for there were many thumb prints on the margin.

"What do you make of it?" asked Dane, frankly puzzled.

Haynes chuckled softly.

"I know what it is all about—but who is the man?" he asked.

Dane stared at him.

"Which man? The man who did the shooting?"

Haynes shook his head.

At that moment the telephone bell rang and Dane answered.

"Yes?" he said, and listened.

Presently he put the instrument down.

"Will you be so kind as to see the head of the Russian Military Mission?" he repeated. "He has given orders that you shall be admitted immediately."

A few minutes later a part of the mystery was solved.

The head of the Russian Mission came straight to the point.

"I have just received information that one of my agents has been killed," he said. "There is a reference to the happening in the stop-press columns of the evening papers."

"Metchiffski?" asked Haynes quietly. "Was he one of your people?"

"A very valuable one," nodded the other, "the matter concerns you personally, as well as your department. Three weeks ago Metchiffski reported to our Intelligence that he was on the track of a big enemy move of some kind. He believed that it was being engineered by the German Foreign Office. Last week he reported that the scheme was elaborated and needed one final touch. He was working hand in hand with the conspirators. He then described the plot as being criminal rather than political. He was an extremely reticent man and never acquainted us with the development of his schemes until they fructified. To-day I received a phone call and I, myself, answered it. I heard Metchiffski's voice say, 'Warn Major Haynes. I am suspect.' His voice was unusually agitated. 'They agreed to try my method but it has failed. They will try their own. He must be careful of Foreign Office letters.' and that was all. I remember every word he said and I know it finished at 'Foreign Office letters.' His voice stopped suddenly. I heard some sort of commotion, but no other sound from the poor fellow."

"Have you any idea as to the nature of the conspiracy?" asked Haynes.

"None whatever," replied the Russian.

"Do you know that he engaged a thief to steal my pocket-book?"

"He must have had an excellent reason," replied the general with a smile. "He had his own peculiar method of working—not always a legal method, I am afraid. He was, as I say, reticent and mystifying. It was his principal fault."

Haynes returned to his bureau and spent the rest of the afternoon in close conference with his assistant.

"It is pretty clear what happened," he said, "for some reason or other the plotters needed my pocket-book, and two alternative methods were suggested. Metchiffski's was the gentler. The other suggested by the unknown gentleman was, I gather, something rather sticky. Metchiffski's failed, and his failure coincided with the discovery by the unknown gang that he was betraying them. They shot him on the evidence of their ears—they overheard him telephoning to the Russian Embassy. By the way, has Scotland Yard made a report on the thumb-prints yet?"

Dane passed a long blue envelope across the table, and Major Haynes extracted and studied the contents with more than ordinary interest.

In a fourth-floor back room off Shaftesbury Avenue—a room which was particularly grimy and unsavory—a man sat reading aloud from three sheets of typescript. Every now and again his shaking hand would stray to a tumbler of cloudy white liquid which stood at his elbow, and at odd intervals he would stop, replenish his glass from a green bottle, and pour water into the liquor drop by drop.

On the other side of the table, his hands thrust into his trousers pockets, was a burly man, evidently of foreign extraction who watched the proceedings with a sneer which he did not attempt to conceal.

"You take a long time to study—yes?" he growled. "To me it is very simple. To you, an actor, it seems very difficult."

"I wish I had never taken the job on," whimpered the man gulping at his glass.

The other laughed.

"You get plenty of money—yes? You are very poor—yes? Also, the police are constantly behind you saying, 'This is Horace Goold, the once great actor.'"

"Oh, shut up," said the man fretfully. "It's a beastly job, I tell you. Suppose this other fellow turns up in Switzerland?"

"You will be in a neutral country. They can do nothing to you," said the burly man smoothly. "Once you are in Switzerland, you are safe, my friend. As to Major Haynes turning up, it is extremely unlikely." His smile was very confident. "You have many advantages, my friend. In the first place, you look like Major Haynes. I do not think in your uniform anybody would know you apart."

Mr. Goold returned to his studies with a groan. There was a time when the name of Horace Goold carried some weight in theaterland, but drink and the morphia habit had wrecked him physically, morally and socially.

He sat, an abject figure, with the light-scared eyes and the uncleanly hands which is the peculiar mark of the dope fiend, fingering his chin indecisively.

Later in the evening he would be a new man, for his eyes would sparkle, his hollow cheeks fill, his body straighten with that stimulant to which he was a slave. For the moment, however, this relief was denied to him by his companion, whose presence in the room was accounted for by this desire of Goold's employers to keep him straight for the day.

The big man had opened his mouth to speak, when there was a commotion on the stairs, the door was flung open and a youth burst into the room.

"Horace," he gasped, "beat it! They're after you."

"After me?" The trembling man stared at the newcomer with lackluster eyes.

"The police," said the youth, "I saw two splits at the corner, and there's two up the street. I heard one of 'em mention your name."

The burly man had turned a shade paler but he retained his presence of mind. He gripped Goold by the arm, and they passed through the door, down one flight of stairs and along a corridor which connected with a workshop at the rear of the premises. He was evidently no stranger to the house, for he unlocked a door which gave to a small paved yard.

As he hustled the shaking man into the yard he heard a sharp knock on the front door and the shuffle of feet of the landlady as she went to answer.

The big man closed the door and the lock snapped.

"We can get through the shop into Wardour Street," he said quickly, "our friend Haynes is a little too late."

"I wish he hadn't been," whined the wreck. "God, I'm dying for a drink!"

Haynes dined at home that night, and had hardly reached the coffee stage when the expected summons came.

It was in the form of a letter bearing the familiar superscription, "Secret and very urgent," and was an order to report immediately "to the undersigned on a matter of the most urgent and confidential nature."

It bore the signature of an under-secretary, and the note was headed with the simple embossed crest of the Foreign Office.

Haynes read it through, put on his overcoat, for the night was wet and chill, and joined the bearer of the letter, who was waiting by a taxicab.

"Mr. Delavere sent the cab for you, sir," said the man, who wore the uniform of a Foreign Office messenger.

"All right, you needn't wait," said Haynes. He opened the door and stepped in.

An hour later a bell rang in the luxurious flat of Mr. Sven Isodor. Mr. Isodor, for very particular reasons, was all alone, and opened the door himself. A man in military uniform stood in the doorway.

A casual observer or even one who knew Major Haynes passing well might with every reason have thought that it was Haynes they now saw. His resemblance to the counter-espionage officer evoked the grudging admiration even of so severe a critic as Mr. Isodor, who closed the door behind the visitor.

Mr. Isodor led the way to his study.

"Sit down and let's have a look at you. You'll do," he approved, as he splashed whisky into a tumbler and sent the soda sizzling in its wake. "Keep to whisky and avoid morphia, and you'll be a man as well as an actor."

"I don't want your advice," snarled the other, raising the glass to his lips with a shaking hand.

"What happened to Haynes? Did they get him?" asked Isodor seating himself.

"I shouldn't be here if they hadn't," replied the visitor sulkily.

"Did he give any trouble?"

"How do I know? I wasn't in the cab. All I know is that I've got his credentials. It's a rotten business."

Mr. Isodor leaned forward.

"Now listen to me. Mr What's-your-name, you've been coached in this part and you've got to go through with it. Your neck's in the rope if you don't. I'm speaking to you as a friend. I hate violence, and murder makes me sick, and you'll understand that I had nothing to do with Metchiffski—the dirty hound—or Haynes."

"Is Haynes dead?" demanded the visitor in a startled voice.

Mr. Isodor waved the question aside.

"That's nothing to do with you or me. I'm only financing the crowd, and they're a pretty tough crowd, I can tell you. Dead or not, he's out of the way. You're Haynes and don't forget it. You leave to-morrow morning by the leave train for France. I've got your diplomatic passport and letters of recommendation. You'll go straight through France to Switzerland. Your tickets are here. You will stay at the Kaiserhof, in Lucerne, and there you'll meet Herr von Keller, and you'll discuss terms of peace. Von Keller will give you a document to sign and you'll sign it. That document will be the draft agreement made between you as a political officer and Von Keller on behalf of the German Government.

"It is the draft of a peace convention which leaves France in the cart. Von Keller will take the document to Germany and it will be published in the German papers—you will stay on in Switzerland. When the British Government repudiates the agreement, you will make a statement that you acted on behalf of the Government, and as you are well known in France your statement will be believed by the French, and there ought to be a clean break between France and Britain. The French will think the British are trying to double-cross them."

"Oh, rubbish!" said the man peevishly. "You don't suppose they'll take my word!"

Mr Isodor clucked his thick lips impatiently.

"Nobody will believe what Horace Goold, a third-rate actor, says," he said deliberately. "Nobody will believe what a morphia maniac says or what a jail bird says; but they'll believe Haynes, and you're Haynes. It is because you look like Haynes that we chose you, and are paying you £500 a week. You're Haynes—you damned fool, don't you understand?"

"Oh, shut up," said the man weakly, "of course, I understand—give me another whisky."

"You've got to sit tight in Switzerland and do nothing except write the letters which will be handed to you to copy. Perhaps you'll write a book—it's already written for you. Your job is to create an atmosphere of suspicion in France."

"Very clever!" murmured the man on the sofa. He was sitting bolt upright, and his air of wretched weariness had vanished. "One of the most artistic bits of work I've ever had to examine. Really, Mr. Isodor, you're rather wonderful. And all that stuff in the exercise book, 'A few American phrases,' 'Patronising and witty,' &c., are notes on my peculiar characteristics."

"Here—" Mr. Isodor was rising to his feet when the other waved him down.

"Keep quiet, my friend," said the visitor, smiling, "and don't turn pale at the sight of a little pistol—you've got one murder to your credit and nearly two. Do not add suicide to your many crimes."

"Who are you?" croaked Isodor.

"Me? Oh, I'm Haynes. You've been telling me so for the past half-hour. You thought I was the actor, but I'm not. I acted the dope-fiend rather well though, didn't I? All your friends are in custody. They were in the cab waiting for me to step in through the door. Unfortunately six of my men were also waiting to step in, too—by the other door. So they were all caught, and some of them were hurt. I arrested the actor this afternoon, just as his guardian angel thought he had escaped—identified him by his thumb prints—and the poor devil blurted most of the story."

Major Haynes jerked his pallid prisoner to his feet.

"Put out your hands, Isodor—it's the long, long trail for yours."

CHAPTER VI

THE TREASURE HOUSE OF THE PRUSSIAN KING

Major Hayes found a peculiar joy in reading the advertisement columns of the daily press in the week which followed March 7. The widow who wanted to sell "between seven and nine" fish knives, the business man who was willing in his spare time to balance tradesmen's books "between seven and nine—except Fridays," the offer of bed sitting rooms to those who would call "between seven and nine," all these and many others containing the cyphers seven and nine in conjunction filled him with chuckling merriment. For those words "between seven and nine" were the S.O.S. signals of innumerable agents, big and little, who veiled their identities behind initials, and box numbers, and meant "no money has been received."

This was very likely true, because the eminent Greek financier, M. Coropulos, was under lock and key, his bank balance under the fatherly care of the Public Trustee, and his elegant business premises in the hands of the police. In other words, by a daring coup Haynes had arrested the chief paymaster of the Imperial German Intelligence Service.

"The animals are waiting to be fed—it's past feeding time, and they're surely raising pitiful cries," said Haynes unsympathetically.

Captain Dane favoured him with one of his rare smiles. "They'll find a new paymaster—I'll bet there's one on his way to Britain at this moment."

Haynes shook his head. "There's one here—if he can get at the money," he said. "No, I don't know who it is. Anyway, it is certain that somebody in this country besides Coropulos has a list of the agents."

"Has he the money?"

"No. The German is not a fool where money is concerned. The second man will act in case of emergency, and the emergency has arisen. Evidently there's a hitch—hence these tearful advertisements. The hitch, I should imagine, is in locating the money."

"You believe it is here?" asked Dane.

"Certain," said the other promptly, "not only money, but arms and explosives in pretty considerable quantities. The German is a beast, but a thorough beast. He anticipated this war, and made his arrangements accordingly. He took steps to meet any contingency which might arise, and he is certain to have established a little Spandau Tower in Britain—a treasure-house for emergencies. Probably even Coropulos knows nothing about it—that would be planted by the top men of the German Intelligence Department. Nobody in Britain would know where it is—the information will have to be sent either from Germany or America. The man here probably knows the method which was adopted in hiding the money, but has no exact information as to its locale. That is how I read the situation."

Dane nodded.

"Of course they won't try to send particulars through by the ordinary channels," he said; "they'd guess we'd suspect existence of the cache, and they'd be scared sick at the idea of the information coming to us. We'll be on the safe side and tighten the postal censorship."

"Couldn't be tighter," said Haynes; "they'll find another way. I'd give twenty million pounds to know what is in von Schiff's mind."

It was a habit of Haynes, to offer fabulous sums for an exposition of von Schiff's secret thoughts—a safe enough offer since that furtive gentleman never left the office in Berlin, where he pulled the strings of twenty espionage services, except to sleep.

There followed days and nights of arrests. The counter-Espionage Bureau left little to chance. The German Spy Service was momentarily paralysed and thrown out of gear. It was the task of the Bureau to make that paralysis permanent. Men and women suspects were "pulled in," questioned and detained. The experts who examine foreign mail matter tested every letter for secret writing, carefully conned every piece of printed matter that came into the country, but without result.

Some fifteen days after Haynes formed his opinion there arrived on the shores of Britain—it would be a misnomer to describe them as "hospitable" at the moment—a young American adventurer, one Barnstable O. Burton.

There is little doubt that Barnstable O. Burton was an idealist; there is less doubt that he was young. He was further handicapped by being in love. He had left Cincinnati in the spring of 1916 with the irrevocable determination to be worthy the callow trust and affections of Miss Lisa Mae Blurtemburg and strike a blow for the Fatherland.

It was not his Fatherland, but he had adopted it for the time being preparatory to marrying into the great Teutonic family; Lisa Mae and he had sat on the stoep through innumerable twilights reading German poetry, and Barnstable O. Burton had gone German in very much the same way as men in the islands go native. He had cast off his reasonable broadcloth, had stuck flowers in his hair, hung a wreath of human teeth about his neck, and, grasping a machete, had gone to the east on a headhunting expedition. These, of course, are figures of speech. In reality Barnstable O. Burton had packed his grip and booked his passage for Liverpool, his head buzzing with instructions which had been imparted to him by a Herr Schlitz and his pocket bulging with wealth.

These instructions were curious. There were, of course, the written orders which he was to digest and destroy on the voyage:—

1. Visit all large military centres. Discover number of troops in training; average length of service; whether men are brigaded in divisional units or are held as drafts.

2. Visit Clyde and report on conditions of labour; number of shipyards working short time; difficulties of securing steel.

3. Visit and report all new Government munition works in process of erection; how far advanced, &c.

Twenty-five clauses on these lines were quite enough for a growing lad to memorise, but two days before he sailed Herr Schlitz sent for him in some agitation

"Mr Burton," he said, "your instructions you may forget—you shall do nothing but stay in London until you receive a visit from a certain doctor. He will tell you that he has called by appointment, and you will take him to your room and he will examine the secret mark which we shall put upon you. After that you may return. This, however, you must understand seriously—you will take no risks. To-night I will bring you to a famous and illustrious doctor, who will make a tattoo mark on your back. It will be painful, but it must be borne. It may save our cause—also it is an order which has been received by wireless."

Barnstable listened and thrilled. It was all so delightfully adventurous, the sort of thing you read about in books. He met the illustrious doctor, and much of the glory and honour of the enterprise evaporated under the electric needle. But Barnstable stuck it like a hero, and slept face downward for a week.

Lisa Mae saw him off, kissed him affectionately on both cheeks and waved an American flag which had a little black eagle surreptitiously embroidered amongst the stars, and Barnstable O. had waved back, his eyes moist with tears, and his heart nigh bursting with love and pride and importance. Also his back hurt like blazes, but somehow this added to the novelty and enjoyment of the moment.

He came to Britain a very-well-off young man—but a young man. He was not content to enjoy himself and take no risks. He had memorised too well the twenty-five clauses of his instructions, and after a week of inaction he began what was undoubtedly a wholly unofficial and unauthorised tour of investigation.

In consequence, he was absent from London when a suave foreign gentleman called at his hotel by appointment—a foreign gentleman who carried a stethoscope in his pocket and was genuinely annoyed to discover that Barnstable O. was away from home.

Barnstable O. did not know this. He was very busily engaged in collecting data about the strength of the British reserves in England. And that is why a month later Barnstable O. was sitting, stunned and bewildered, in a grey stone cell in the Tower of London, listening but not understanding the findings of the Court-Martial, monotonously recited by a grave old officer.

"The Court finds the prisoner, Barnstable Oliver Burton, a citizen of the United States of America, guilty of an act of espionage, and, further of attempting to seduce the allegiance of His Majesty's Forces in that he did, on the third day of April, 1916, endeavour to obtain information regarding the disposition of His Majesty's troops by offering a bribe to a member of His Majesty's Forces, to wit, Sergeant Thomas Dohetty, of the King's Dragoon Guards, to supply him with a return . . . the Court sentences Barnstable Oliver Burton to be shot until he is dead, and his body to be buried within the precincts of the place of his execution."

"You understand, my boy?" said the old officer gently.

"Yes, sir," said Barnstable O. huskily. "When—when will this be?"

"On Monday morning at daybreak—that is, in six days' time. You will have every facility to communicate with the American Embassy, and you may, of course, write whatever letters you wish . . ."

"Thank you, sir," said Barnstable O.

The steel door swung to with a "hush" of air and the boy was left alone to the clamour and confusion of is thoughts.

On the third day of his supreme trial the cell door opened, and a lithe, lean-faced officer came in, closing the door behind him.

Barnstable O looked up at the officer and stood up.

"Sit down," said Major Haynes of the Counter-Espionage Bureau. "I've come to have a little talk with you."

"I didn't recognise you." The boy smiled faintly. "You're the officer—"

"Who pinched you—yes, I am that same sleuth," said Haynes. "Well, what do you think of things?"

Barnstable ran his fingers through his hair. "I guess I've been rather a fool," he said, and Haynes nodded.

"Ever go fishing?" he asked.

"Yes, I did a lot back home."

"What do you do with the half-grown fish that you catch?"

"Throw 'em back," said the boy.

Haynes nodded again.

"That's what's going to happen to you, young Barnstable O. We're going to throw you back into your element."

"What!"

The boy was on his feet, his face drawn and white.

"There's a steamer leaves a certain British port for a certain Atlantic port—I won't deceive you, it's from Liverpool for New York—on Saturday. You go with it, because my paternal Government think you are too young for the beastly business of a firing party."

The boy was silent.

"That's fine," he said after a while. "When do I—leave here?"

"In time to catch the boat—your belongings are already en-route to Liverpool. Now look, I'm not going to give you any advice. We don't ask you to be anything except a good American citizen, and that's dead easy to an honest man. We do not ask you to betray any secrets which your friends confided in you, nor do we ask you to run a lecture tour on the benevolence of the British Government—you've just got to be a good boy."

"One thing more," said Haynes, "you have on your back a tattooed design which resembles, as far as I can make out from the photograph, an Iron Cross with divers hieroglyphics. Will you tell me the circumstances under which you came into possession of that work of art?"

"Tell me this," he went on, "was the tattooing an eleventh hour scheme?"

"Yes—it was done at the last moment."

"Can you remember the date; was it about March 7 or 8?"

"It was on March 8," said Barnstable promptly. "I remember the date because it was my birthday."

"One more question. Was the man who did the tattooing a doctor, and did his name begin with A?"

The boy hesitated, and Haynes smiled.

"Dr Albrecht was arrested by the U.S. Secret Service the day after you sailed," he said quietly. "He hanged himself in his cell—if it were he you need have no fear."

"It was he," said Barnstable O.

"The last request, son," smiled Haynes. "Let me see this grand little totem of yours."

The boy stripped his coat. The man who did the marking was an artist, for the impression was clear and good.

"H'm," said Haynes, "an Iron Cross with the German motto 'Gott mit uns.' What is the Celtic Cross, I wonder, and who is Smith, and what does 7.1.13 mean? And what is the queer little design underneath?"

"I cannot tell you," said the boy ruefully. "If I could I think I would."

Haynes dropped his hand on his shoulder. "Barnstable O.," he said, "you've had your lesson. Be a good boy."

He shook hands with a speechless lad and parted, to meet him again on Princes Landing Stage on the following Saturday afternoon.

Barnstable O. had recovered something of his old spirits, something of the buoyancy which had been his when he left the United States. But for the lines at the corner of his eyes—there to remain for the term of his natural life, although this was not part of the Court Martial's sentence—he was in appearance all that you might expect a youth of 18 to be.

"I've seen Mr Carter from our Embassy," he said, "and he told me that I owe my life to you, Major Haynes. I'll never forget it, sir, never. Some day—"

"Oh, shut up, Barnstable O." said Haynes hastily.

Before the boat left Haynes saw two of the passengers, quiet, unobtrusive men, who carried no outward and visible sign of their connection with the United States Secret Service.

"Boys," said he, "you've just got to watch that lad day and night: The first passenger on board who turns the conversation in the direction of tattoo markings before the boat is out of sight of the land you will arrest—if necessary signal a patrol boat and hand him over. Nobody must see the markings on that youth under any circumstances. If you're stopped by a U-boat you are to take him forcibly and paint his back blue so that the design is hidden."

He explained in a few words the significance of the "secret mark."

"It's an old idea—Haggard worked it in one of his books, 'Mr Meeson's Will'—and the Hun is some student!"

He watched the ship swing into the mystery of grey seas.

It had been part of Haynes' business to trace all the people who had been associated directly or indirectly with Barnstable O. in the period between his arrival in the country and his arrest, and he had not omitted to note the arrival at Barnstable's hotel of a distinguished-looking foreigner who ostentatiously displayed a stethoscope. At first he had been inclined to believe that this was a genuine medical visitation. Afterwards when he realised what the visit of the doctor signified he made a diligent search for the man, without, however, achieving any discovery.

He did not doubt that already the secret of the treasure house was on its way to England. Two nights after the departure of Barnstable a solitary enemy aeroplane flew over the East Coast defences, and was duly shelled, and disappeared into the interior. It was a fine moonlight night, and the coast watchers waited for its return, but to their surprise no sound of engines was heard, and their surmise that it had come down was accurate, but it had been a voluntary if unfortunate landing, for it descended in a field adjacent to the camp of the 34th West Riding Regiment, and the pilot was captured after a desperate struggle, in the course of which he endeavoured to destroy an envelope which he was carrying. This was duly forwarded to Haynes the next morning, and, as he expected, it was a replica of the design on Barnstable's back.

Whether the pilot had mistaken the signals or whether the man who was waiting to receive the message had himself inadvertently taken up his position near a camp Haynes could only guess. Inquiries elicited the fact that a man answering to the description furnished by the hotel servants as being identical with the "doctor" had boarded a train three miles away from the place where the aeroplane fell, and had gone in the direction of London. An abandoned bicycle was found on the roadside, but there were no other clues to his identity.

"It is not the last attempt that will be made," said Haynes, and that he was right was demonstrated that night when he was called from his bed to answer a 'phone call.

It was Dane's voice speaking at the other end.

"Is that you, Haynes? A man landed from the inward American mail to-day carrying a trunk covered with labels."

Haynes' swore softly.

"And under one of the labels was the design. I ought to have foreseen that. Have you got the man?"

"He has been arrested, but unfortunately it was too late."

"The doctor had seen him?" asked Haynes.

"Yes," came the answer; "the man drove straight to the Bertland Hotel. It was the chambermaid who saw him carefully stripping a label, and, thinking it was strange, communicated with the police. The Liverpool police got there just too late."

"I will be at the office in ten minutes," said Haynes, and dressing hastily, he drove through the deserted streets to the War Office.

He found Dane sitting with an enlarged photograph of the design.

"I've had a 'phone message from Liverpool since I called you," he said; "it appears that ten minutes after the doctor had arrived the bell was very violently rung, and the doctor asked for a Bradshaw. The curious thing was that when he was told that the Bradshaw was not up to date he replied impatiently that any date would do."

"H'm," said Haynes, "so he wanted to see something which is in every Bradshaw irrespective of its date. Obviously he was not looking out the time of a train."

He looked at the design and whistled.

"What a fool I've been!" he said, and pointed to the letters at the top of the cross. "'B.R.D.W' means 'Bradshaw,' the 'LII' stands for 'Page 52,' which means that it is part of the index."

Dane rose and took a Bradshaw and laid it on the table.

"Page 52," said Haynes, turning the leaves quickly. "The 4. I presume, stands for Column 4, and the 11 for the eleventh line. That is pretty elementary. 'Newton Abbot.' So our treasure house is somewhere near Newton Abbot! But where and what is the Iron Cross for and the 'Gott mit uns.' and what is that infernal design at the bottom."

He paced up and down the room, his head upon his breast. Presently he looked up.

"Get through to Paddington. I want a special train to Newton Abbot," he said, "in half an hour. Collect all the survey maps of South Devonshire you can and come along with me. By the way, what time was this arrest made?"

"Eight o'clock," said Dane, and Haynes groaned.

"Eight o'clock." he said in despair, "and it is now 12.50. He has got four and a half hours' start, and could easily have caught the Southern express, which lands him in Newton somewhere about three o'clock in the morning."

Half an hour later he was driving down the decline into Paddington Station.

"We have about four and a half hours to solve the mystery of this iron cross," said Haynes when the train had fairly started on its journey.

The table in the big saloon was outspread with the survey maps which Dane had brought, and Haynes was slowly tracing a circle about Newton Abbot.

"I confess that the cross baffles me," said Dane.

"The 'B.R.D.W.' baffled us too," said Haynes calmly. "We shall probably find the other is just as simple. By-the-way, what do you expect is the solution?"

Dane scratched his ear solemnly.

"I expect we shall find some place bearing this mark. That sounds weak, but any of my theories are rather feeble. Who is Smith, by the way, and what is that weird design at the bottom?"

Haynes did not reply He had stopped listening, and his fingers were now moving slowly and patiently over a limited area of the map. He jotted down a few notes, and took up a handbook of Devon which he had brought with him, and after consulting the index turned up the page, and for ten minutes was deeply immersed in his reading.

Presently he closed the book, put it down on the table, folded up the maps, and replaced them in their leather satchel. He took out a long cigar, lit it, and settled himself comfortably in the lounge chair which formed part of the furniture of the car.

"If you are awake call me at Exeter, Dane."

"All this is beautifully mysterious," said Dane irritably; "but do I understand that you have found a solution?"

"Practically," said the other. "The treasure is hidden at Willbury-in-the-Moor, a charming little village some five miles from Newton."

"Wonderful man," said Dane sarcastically. "Will you condescend to enlighten me as to how you arrived at this conclusion?"

But Haynes was asleep and genuinely so, for he had the gift of sleeping at will.

At Newton Abbot three cars were waiting, two of which were occupied by members of the local constabulary. Haynes shook hands with the officer in charge of the police and gave brief directions, and the party went through the deserted streets of the market town as the first flushes of dawn appeared in the eastern skies.

There was a motor trolley at the corner of the cross roads of Willbury-in-the-Moor as the three cars came into the village. It was drawn up outside the entrance to the ancient churchyard, and at the moment of Haynes' appearance four men carrying a long and sombre object were passing through the lych gate.

Haynes jumped clear of the car, a pistol in each hand.

"I won't ask you to put up your hands because that would be unreasonable," he said in German, "but the first man that reaches for his pocket will be much deader than the late Herr Smith."

The vicar of Willbury-in-the-Moor was a startled man when he was roused from his sleep at daybreak and found himself confronted by two unshaven officers, one of whom needed no introduction, for the fame of Haynes was wide.

"I am sorry to bother you, vicar," said Haynes, "but I want a little information."

"I shall be most happy to give it," said the startled cleric.

"Two years ago you had a man named Smith in your parish who died here?"

The vicar nodded.

"Do you know anything about him?"

"I remember the case very well," said the vicar. "He came here two months before his death, and was, I believe, a great invalid. He occupied a furnished house in the village, and few people saw him except his servant and his medical attendant."

"Was Smith an Englishman?"

"It is curious you should ask that," said the vicar. "As a matter of fact, I believe he was a German, and that his name was Schmidt. He was a very rich man, and had a wish to die in this beautiful spot."

"And he accordingly died," said Haynes brusquely and a little brutally it seemed to Dane, "and his death was certified by his medical attendant and he was buried?"

"In a vault," said the vicar, "which he had had built two months before his death."

"Which occurred," said Haynes, "on the 7th January, 1913. Would you know the doctor again if you saw him?"

"Oh, yes," said the vicar. "I should remember him very well."

"Bring him in," said Haynes, and Dane went away and brought back a somewhat dishevelled man, whose wrists were securely fastened in steel manacles.

"That is the man," said the vicar.

"Thank you," said Haynes, "that clears up everything. Of course, I knew most of it. The only doubt I had was as to the method they adopted to secure a burial."

"What do you mean?" asked the vicar.

Haynes smiled.

"I only mean, sir, that nobody was ever buried in that vault. Smith never died. The handsome casket which was laid so reverently to rest behind the steely bars of Mr Smith's vault contained something over £400,000 in English bank notes, innumerable books of instructions and codes, and a great deal of other matter which probably interests me more than it does you."

He jerked his head, and they took the prisoner out.

"It was the iron cross which led us astray," said Haynes, "the tiny cross on the left-hand corner, of course, stood for a burial place."

"But how did you locate the treasure house at Willbury-in-the-Moor?" asked Dane, mystified.

"I repeat," said Haynes, "it was the cross which led us astray. It is really a map of four cross roads, in the corner of which stands a church. That was obvious. The locale was specially chosen by the ingenious German, who is a thorough beast, less for its remoteness than for the curious fact that the road on the left leads to the village of Gottleigh, that on the right to the village of Mittchfield, and that on the south to the village of Unstover or Little Unstover as it is called. As a matter of fact, this was known to our clever doctor. What he was waiting for was the key. The vault has a very complicated lock, and I should imagine that it is almost impossible to open the two gates without the use of dynamite. That curious little design at the bottom which puzzled us both is an exact drawing of the wards of a key. The curious thing that looks like a note of exclamation on the right is a section of the key."

"But wouldn't the doctor know all about the key and the secret of the vault?"

Haynes shook his head.

"Only one man knew that, and that man was Smith, who was officially dead, but who superintended his own funeral with the greatest care and forethought," he said, "You see, what happened was this. They brought the alleged Smith down to the village. He hid himself in a house, had his own medical attendant, and industriously circulated the report that he was dying. In the course of time he passed away, having first caused to be built you may be sure, by German workmen, a vault in which the money was to be hidden away against a rainy day. When the right moment arrived he departed this life, his death was certified by his attendant, and he was buried without the full military honours to which he was entitled, for I suspect Smith was our dear old friend Von Schiff himself. The doctor only knows where the money is hidden. He had in his possession ten keys, all very similar in shape and design, but only one fitting the lock of the vault, which, as I say, was a complicated one, and so designed that any attempt to force it or the employment of the wrong key would automatically jam the mechanism."

Still Dane was not convinced.

"But if the doctor knew where the treasure was located," he said obstinately, "why take the trouble to include the iron cross at all; why not just simply send a sketch of the key or the number of the key?"

Haynes nodded.

"I've been thinking of that myself," he said, "and I can come to only one conclusion, that this is not the only treasure house in Britain, and I am going to set myself the task of finding the other locks that the nine keys fit. I don't suppose this is the first time Smith has been buried!"

CHAPTER VII

THE QUESTION OF HORA DA SILVA

"What do you think it is worth?"

The stout, bald man, who puffed regularly at his cigar did not take his eyes from his companion as he asked the question.

He sat in a deep arm chair, near enough to the table to reach for the little pile of papers he had laid near its edge, but at a sufficient distance to avoid the direct rays of the shaded electric lamp which stood on the table.

His visitor seemed no less anxious to keep in the shadow. He sat on a low chair, his head down; his nervous fingers clasping and unclasping between his knees.

"It's worth—a lot," he said doggedly. "You're asking me to do—a lot. This country may become a bit too hot for me, even if it wasn't found out."

"What do you think it is worth?" asked the stout man again.

The other moved uneasily.

"You know the hole I'm in. I owe over a thousand pounds, and I never thought—"

The stout man chuckled.

"Gamblers never think or they wouldn't gamble," he laughed, and the other looked up with a scowl. ,

"Look here! I don't want any moralising from you! Good God! Isn't it bad enough that I should be seeing you at all, knowing what I know—a Government servant negotiating with a spy—it's awful."

The stout man rubbed his nose impatiently. It was one of those gestures which, for some inexplicable reason, accompanies a sudden irritation of mind.

"Don't pity yourself, my friend—help yourself," he said. "You owe a thousand which you lost at a gambling house in London—good, or bad, as the case may be. Your creditors are pressing you, and you are afraid that the matter will come to the ears of your chief—good again. You answer a moneylender's advertisement and get deeper into trouble, and the moneylender asks you to do him a favour which will do you no harm, will free you from debt, and put a thousand or so in your pocket."

He paused, and the man looked up.

"Go on," he growled.

He of the cigar stretched out his hand and took a paper from the top of the pile.

"Ruth da Silva!" he read. "I won't trouble to read her description, because you'll see her in ten minutes—widow of Joseph Marie da Silva, an Eurasian of Bedgaum in the Province of Madras. That is your lady, my friend; now I will tell you something about her."

He put down the paper and settled himself in his chair.

"Joseph da Silva is the only Eurasian of note who was ever concerned in an anti-British plot in India. He was a clever and capable man, a good speaker, and a born organiser. I say 'was' because he is dead, having been assassinated by Ramhal Bjendi, who was hung at Poona for the murder. In every way the murder was a folly, even though da Silva had gone back on the conspirators and had betrayed one of them in one of those spasms of patriotism to which half-breed people are susceptible. It was the white in him which responded to the call of his country, I suppose but at any rate he went to the Government in the summer of 1915 and was killed. The murder was a mistake, because da Silva was the man through whose hands passed all the correspondence with an important—indeed the most important—branch of the Conspirators' League in San Francisco. You know, of course, that the American police have arrested the leaders of the movement in California, and that the Indian police have also rounded up the leaders in Calcutta, Delhi, and Bombay?"

The visitor nodded.

"What you may not know is that there is a branch in Britain. Da Silva knew; in fact there was very little he did not know. If you have read the reports of the various trials you cannot fail to be impressed by the fact that the police, both in India and San Francisco, have had very little documentary evidence to go upon. They have been obliged to rely upon informers. The reason is simple. Save for letters, written in the most carefully guarded terms, there are no documents or records. That was where da Silva was invaluable. He had an extraordinary memory. It is said that he could read a column from a newspaper once and repeat every word he had read. The records of the society were inside his head. He knew the names of agents, the amount of their monthly stipends, and it may be said that when he died the records of the society were destroyed. Most disastrous of all, he carried to the grave the one secret which the society could not afford to lose. He alone knew who were the four or five rich Hindoos who were financing the movement."

He sucked reflectively at his cigar.

"You understand that those four or five men contributed large sums monthly. They were important and influential men, some of them holding high positions in India. After the murder their contributions ceased; they were probably scared sick. Now, the loss of the money is of minor importance to my friends, whatever it may be to the Indian gentlemen engaged in the—er—political movement. The loss of their identity is serious. If we could go boldly to them and say 'Mr So-and-So, we have proof that you were parties to a conspiracy, etc.' we could use them for other purposes. It is only sufficient that we should know their names—it is your job to discover those names for me."

"But how?"

"By any method which ingenuity suggests. You are a Government official; you might terrorise or threaten or cajole."

He looked at his watch.

"Her train is due to arrive in twenty minutes, and we must be at the station so that I can point her out to you. One word more. I am not the only person, and you will not be the only person engaged in wheedling this secret from the lady."

"Does she know?"

The man with the cigar nodded.

"Da Silva was passionately devoted to his Irish wife, and I know that she shared many of his secrets. It is certain that on more occasions than one she was the actual messenger who brought the money. I was saying that, we are not the only people who are trying to discover the secret. You should know that I am working independently of the Indians, who are after the money only. In addition, I have reason to believe that a department of the Austrian Government is pursuing investigations probably on behalf of the Turkish Government, which is interested in discovering the names of its friends in India."

The two men rose together, and the stouter and shorter of the two struggled into a light dustcoat, threw his cigar into the fireplace, and pulled on his gloves. The other stood for some time looking at the carpet deep in thought.

"It doesn't strike me you are paying very highly," he said, "considering the services you expect and what would be my position after. How do I know that you won't find it convenient to use your knowledge of what I have done to my detriment?"

The little man laughed quietly.

"You are hardly big enough for us," he smiled, and the visitor swallowed the insult with a gulp.

Ten minutes later they stood by the barrier at the big railway station and watched the stream of passengers flowing forth. Presently the little man nudged the other.

"There she is," he whispered.

A woman, quietly dressed, tall and good-looking, passed through the barrier, looking neither to the left nor right, and the bigger man eyed her keenly.

"I've got her," he said. "Where is she going now?"

"She leaves for London by the eight o'clock train to-night. She has been living in Morpeth for the past three months, and I believe we have made it rather uncomfortable for her," he smiled quietly.

He took from his pocket-book a slip of paper and handed it to his companion.

"That will be her address in London."

"34 Golders Tenements," said the other.

"Do you know them?"

"Very well. Not a very expensive residence."

The little man shrugged.

"That woman who has secrets worth hundreds of thousands of pounds—not to us, of course," he corrected himself hastily, "has exactly £1 a week to live on. We have offered to buy her secret, but she professes to know nothing."

That night when Ruth da Silva left Newmarket for London she was shadowed, though this would not have worried her even if she had known, for she had been shadowed since she left India six months before.

Haynes looked up from the letter he was writing as Bayley, the chief of his "watchers," came into the office.

"Oh, Bayley," he said, picking up a slip of paper containing a few words of writing, "here is the alleged name and the certain address of one, Julius B. Merrit, who claims to be an American citizen, and is officially recorded as one at the Embassy. He lives, as you see, at 35 Golders Tenements, Waterloo Bridge Road. I don't want you to interfere with him or to make any inquiries about him. I want him shadowed. He does not usually go abroad until nightfall. He sports a beard—here's a rough sketch of his face, no photograph being available—but the beard is probably false though excellently put on."

"What do you want to know, sir?"

"Where he goes, who he meets, what means of conveyance he has, what letters he receives at other addresses."

"Very good, sir." Bayley was on the move to the door.

"One moment. Golders Tenements have two entrances—one leading to Waterloo Road and one to Cheyne Street. You need to watch the Waterloo Road; he never goes out by the other. It's a one-man job; send Parkson."

"Parkson, sir?" Bayley hesitated. "He's quite well known in that part of London after we pinched the Bickoffs in the borough."

"Send Parkson," said Haynes. "The Bickoffs had no friends," and with a nod he dismissed his subordinate and went on writing his letter.

Captain Dane, working at the other end of the room, waited until Bayley had gone before he asked—

"Who is Merrit, Haynes?"

"An anarchist or something," said Haynes without stopping his writing. "A week ago he moved into Golder's Tenements from nowhere in particular. He is only seen occasionally—once or twice a week—so the possibility is that he really lives somewhere else, and only turns up in Waterloo Road when he is feeling really naughty and anarchistic."

"But," persisted the other, "is he on our list?"

"Yes and no," said Haynes. "Forgive me if I am mysterious and talk like an eminent detective, but mystery is eggs and bacon to me. One of these days I'm going to open a private inquiry office, and woe to the erring husband or the flighty wife."

Dane growled.

"You talk such utter piffle sometimes."

"Why 'sometimes'?" demanded Haynes. "You're getting positively sycophantic!"

He worked all that afternoon, and left to catch the 6.10 to Maidenhead.

"I've taken a cottage on the river. You can run down some night and see me in my more frivolous moments."

"Well, don't I?" snarled Dane, and Haynes was still laughing when he reached Whitehall.

Bayley reported promptly at eleven the next morning.

"Parkson saw your man, sir—he's a rum bird."

"Who—Parkson?" asked Haynes.

"No sir—Merrit."

"Wherein does his rumness lie?"

"Here's the report, sir," Bayley refused to be enticed into an argument with his chief. "Merrit left his home at 10.17. Followed to Elephant and Castle, where he took a tram car to Camberwell. Got into a motor car which was waiting for him and travelled southward. Parkson lost him, but picked him up later returning. Parkson says the beard may be false, but it looks real. He wears rimless glasses and chews gum and Parkson thinks he is an American."

"The gum and the glasses are conclusive evidence," said Haynes gravely. "And after Parkson stopped thinking, did he come to any other conclusion?"

He rose to his feet and stretched himself.

"Ruth da Silva," he said inconsequently.

His subordinate looked puzzled.

"I was mentioning the name of a lady who could probably account for the presence of Mr Merrit in Golder's Tenements. I can tell you something else about him which may interest you, Bayley. He speaks eight languages, and has other qualities. He is a wonderfully good shot with a revolver—quite as good and as quick as I am, if the immodesty be pardoned. In fact, the man who calls himself Merrit—it is not his name, of course—is a particularly intelligent and capable person, and one not lightly to be despised. By the way, I had better see Parkson."

Parkson came in a few minutes, a strongly-built, capable-looking man, who took the chair to which Haynes nodded and sat, balancing his hat in his hand.

"You are watching Merrit?" said Haynes.

"Yes sir, my report—"

"I've seen it," interrupted Haynes, "and I'm not particularly pleased with it."

"I'm sorry, sir. I—"

"Let me finish. You've done good work for us, Parkson; but I seem to detect a falling off in regard to the present job. You lack, if I may say so, the initiative I expected from you. For instance, I see nothing in your report of Mrs Da Silva."

"Mrs Da Silva?"

"She lives, by a curious coincidence, on the same landing as Merrit. Did you know that?"

"I believe that a woman of that name does live there, but what is the significance, sir? I was not told that I must shadow anybody but Merrit. There is no more reason why I should watch her than anybody else in the building."

"Perhaps not," said Haynes, and ended the interview.

"Aren't you a trifle unreasonable?" asked Dane, when the man had gone.

His tone was one of surprise, because Haynes was many things, but he was never unreasonable, and certainly he made the fullest allowance for his subordinates.

"I wonder if I am," said Haynes coolly; "yet it seems to me that Parkson should have known that Mrs Da Silva had two visitors yesterday who left her in a state of considerable agitation. Parkson should have known also that Julius Merritt was a witness to that interview, though none of the three were aware of the fact. Further, Parkson should have known that Mr Merrit himself had an interview with the lady—that is all."

"How do yon know this?" asked Dane. "I realise that it is a silly question to ask since it seems to be your job to know everything, but this time I am curious."

"And this time," said Haynes genially, "I am very mysterious."

"Don't you like Parkson?" insisted Dane.

For a moment Haynes did not reply, then—"Parkson is a pretty good man," he said cautiously, "with the defects of his class. He was a private detective agent until he joined this bureau, and the only private detective that ever did brainy things was Sherlock Holmes, and he was only brainy because he never existed except in the fertile imagination of a novelist."

Dane laughed.

"At any rate you have given Parkson something to do," he said. "The poor beggar will be taking a census of Golder's Tenements to-night."

"Then he will learn a great deal which is interesting," replied Haynes.

Golder's Tenements consisted of a square, ugly block of apartments, divided into four sections distinguished by the first four letters of the alphabet. Each section boasted of an ill-lighted stone staircase which led up to four landings, on each side of which were two doors facing one another.

On the second floor of Block A dwelt the mysterious Mr Merrit, and opposite to him the no less mysterious Mrs da Silva. She had been a beautiful girl, and was still a pretty woman. As she stood in the doorway looking with troubled eyes at the two men who confronted her she bore herself with that odd dignity which is the special possession of the European woman who has maintained her caste through years of married life with one of an inferior race. Not all white women who marry Eurasians retain their pride, but Ruth da Silva was an exception.

She kept her hand on the edge of the door and did not invite her visitors to come

"Why do you come again?" she asked. "I told you last night that I had nothing to tell you."

"Will you not see us for a few moments?" pleaded one of the men.

"I will see you here," she said decisively.

The two exchanged glances, and one uttered a protest.

"I will see you here, she repeated firmly, "or not at all."

"Madam," said the man who had not before spoken, "it is vitally necessary that you should tell us what we asked last night." He lowered his voice until it was a mere rumble of sound to Mr Merrit who, crouched behind the opposite door, his ear to the keyhole, was listening to every word. "There are some who will promise they will pay you better than we, but, madam, there is nothing you can ask for which we will not give you."

"I don't want your money," she replied shortly. "I told you that last night. I don't know the men who subscribed the money, and if I did I would not tell you."

"We do not want to know them all," said one of the men eagerly. "If you could tell us the names of two or even one—"

"She put out her hand with a weary gesture.

"I will tell you none," she said, and tried to close the door, but the man had put his foot inside.

"If you don't go away, I'll scream," she cried desperately; but there was no need to scream, for Merrit's door was wide open. He spoke quickly in a language she did not understand, though she knew it was German. There was a command in his guttural voice, which the men, at any rate, understood. For a minute or two there was a fierce exchange of widespread words and then the two visitors turned and slowly descended the stone stairs.

Mr Julius B. Merrit walked to the edge of the stairs and watched them depart, stroking his flaxen beard reflectively. He turned to the woman in the doorway.

"I am sorry you have been troubled," he said, and she thought she detected the slightest trace of a foreign accent. "So they have come again, eh?"

She nodded, looking at him steadily.

"Perhaps they will not bother you again," he said. "They want to know something, eh?" He looked at her sharply. "They wish to know the names of the Indian gentlemen who contributed so lavishly to the funds of the Indian conspiracy?"

"I know nothing about it," she said shortly.

He shrugged his shoulders.

"You may regard me as your friend," said he. "Perhaps one day you will confide in me—no?"

"I shall confide in nobody," she said.

"That is a very good resolution," he nodded his head approvingly.

"I am very much obliged to you—" she began, but he waved her thanks aside.

"It is nothing—nothing."

They stood in their respective doorways as though both were hesitating to close the door upon one another, and it was the woman who broke the silence.

"I don't know what you want or what you are after," she said. "I know I am getting sick of this, and I shall go to the police if I am bothered any more. I am trying to be loyal to my husband's friends, and I am being persecuted—persecuted—persecuted! They drove me out of Morpeth; they drove me out of Dublin. I have done my best to shake them off, but they follow me everywhere I go. I know you are one of them, though you have been so kind to me, but, Mr Merrit, I will never tell you anything—even if I knew it," she added quickly.

"That is a very good resolution," he said again, and with a little bow closed the door.

He had promised that she should not be bothered again, but his promise was evidently confined to the two men who had interviewed her, for half an hour later there came another knock at the door.

This time it was a stranger, a thick-set man, obviously English.

"Mrs da Silva?" he asked.

"That is my name," she replied.

"I want to see you if you can give me five minutes."

She shook her head.

"I can see nobody," she said.

For answer he took a case from his pocket and produced a card.

"I am Sergeant Parkson, from the Counter-Intelligence Bureau," he said. She looked at the card and opened the door a little wider.

"The police?" she asked.

He nodded.

"I think it is as well you have come," she said wearily. "I have a statement to make which will interest you."

She closed the door behind him and led the way to the little ill-furnished sitting-room and pushed the one easy-chair nearer the table.

"First of all, what do you want of me?"

"I have come to make some inquiries," said Parkson, "in regard, to the Delhi conspiracy. I want to know—"

"You want to know who was concerned in it. You want to know the men who found the money?"

Parkson eyed her keenly.

"That is what I want to know," he said.

"Well, I will tell you."

The detective took out his pocket-book and opened it.

"My husband, as you know, was concerned in this conspiracy, and before his murder was one of the most trusted members of the organisation," she began. "It was he who collected the moneys."

"I know all that," said the detective quickly. "What I want to know is who were the four or five big men in Bombay and Calcutta who financed the movement?"

"First of all," she began, "there was—"

"Don't say it," said a voice in the doorway.

Parkson looked round and jumped to his feet. Mr Julius B. Merrit was closing the door behind him.

"What do you want?" demanded Parkson.

"Many things," said Mr Merrit. "I want the names which Mrs da Silva is about to tell you, but I can wait for that. In the meantime I want you."

"Who are you?" growled Parkson.

The intruder laughed.

"This is where I ought, really to pull off my whiskers and disclose myself," he said, "but, unfortunately, they are glued so tight to me that I must sacrifice the dramatic. I cannot even shed an eyebrow to secure my effect, but my name is Haynes."

Parkson collapsed into the chair.

"You see, Parkson," Haynes went, on, "I happened to know that you were in the hands of moneylenders, and what was more unfortunate for you, I happened to know who those moneylenders were and what they wanted you for. I had to give you an opportunity of carrying out your nefarious work, and at the same time make sure that you did not carry it out to the entire satisfaction of your employer, who, by the way, was arrested this afternoon. Hence these whiskers. You will find Mr Bayley waiting at the foot of the stairs for you with an escort."

Parkson took up his hat and walked slowly from the room.

"Now," said Haynes briskly, "we will have those names from you, Mrs da Silva. There ought to be a hot time in little old Calcutta to night."

CHAPTER VIII

THE ELUSIVE SWEIZER

On a certain morning in May, 1917, a small furniture truck drew up to the front door of No. 475 Bloomsbury Place, and three leisurely men in green baize aprons proceeded with the deliberation of their kind to carry out a piano. A near-by policeman on point duty saw the removal, and duly noted the name and address of the carrier. He observed that no other furniture was taken.

Two detectives of the Anti-Espionage Bureau who were watching the house next door to where the piano was being removed, and had been so watching since the early morning strolled over and in their inquisitive way made inquiries.

The piano was the property of a Sir George Smith, who was the tenant of a flat—No, 475 was let out in this way—and Mr Smith was known in the neighbourhood as a respectable Civil servant. He had removed to Brighton owing to the prevalence of air raids, and had taken his furniture with him, selling the piano to a man to whom he had sub-let his flat in the last months of his tenancy. This much the estate agent at the corner of Bloomsbury Place informed the police officer who made the inquiry.

So the two men of the special detective service went back to their post of observation and signalled to two others at the other end of the street that all was well.

The truck had taken its load, and was disappearing round the corner, when a long grey car swept into the street from Bloomswick Square, and a tall, slight man in uniform sprang out. The detectives saluted him.

"Has he come?" he asked.

"No, sir," replied one of the men.

Major Haynes looked at his watch.

"A quarter-past eleven," he said, and cursed softly.

His curse embraced various heads of public departments, particularly the head of that department which at the moment he was protecting from itself, and the men, who knew the cause of his annoyance, smiled sympathetically and, if the truth be told, admiringly, for Haynes had a vocabulary extensive and lurid.

"I suppose we'll have to do it as this fool Minister wants it done," he said, "though why they couldn't have handed this job over to the regular police and arrested Snape with the goods on him Heaven only knows! Has anybody come out since morning?" he asked.

"No, sir."

"And nobody has gone in?"

"No, sir."

Haynes paced up and down the pavement. "I won't trouble to ask you whether the back of the house is watched," he said once as he came abreast.

Haynes' annoyance was justified. He had been requisitioned at the eleventh hour by the International Department, the sleuths of which had discovered that one of their clerks was undoubtedly keeping questionable company. They had kept him under observation, and had duly observed that he had made two attempts to extract from the safe in which it was kept the most secret and confidential emergency code—that code by which I.D. communicated with their agents in Germany.

Every big public department has its own intelligence staff, and it was the illusion of the I.D. that their particular detective service was something so close to perfection that it rubbed the paint off. The I.D. intelligence were just a little too clever. Had they been very ordinary policemen they would have arrested the young man then and there but they were hypnotised by greater possibilities. They had allowed him rope, hugging to their breasts their precious secret, and only the night before had they communicated in a panic with the bureau to which their troubles should have been communicated in the first place.

Haynes stopped in his walk. "I suppose you fellows know what we are after? Those priceless asses of the I.D. have discovered that Snape has an appointment with the mystery man of 475," he nodded towards the house. "Instead of landing him they are keen on catching him in the act, so to speak."

He swore again. He had been torn away from a close and intimate hunt for Sweizer, who was known to be in London, and Sweizer was a prize worth securing. They called him "the traveller," and certainly his work had been seen in three continents in as many years. To be interrupted in his hunt was bad enough. To be interrupted in order to bring a peccant office boy to justice and to envelope the obvious in a cloak of mystery was maddening.

"Do you expect any trouble, chief?" asked one of the men. "The I.D. people think that this Sweizer—"

"This what?" Haynes wheeled round. It was as though he had been struck in the face. Sweizer was his own private quarry. None knew of his lone hunt. He alone had tracked him from Paris to Lyons, from Lyons back to London.

"Sweizer!" he repeated quickly. "Who said Sweizer was there?"

"The chief of the I.D. service," said the man in surprise.

Haynes drew a long breath.

"And they knew he was there and they just left him! Holy Mike!" He glanced at his watch. "Snape or no Snape, I am going to look at friend Sweizer," he said.

"Here's our man, sir," said one of the officers.

Along the road on the opposite side walk came a somewhat pallid youth, walking with quick, nervous stops, his head bent, his eyes on the ground. He glanced round in terror as Haynes accosted him.

"Reginald Snape," said Haynes.

"No—yes," stammered the young man.

"Make up your mind," said Haynes impatiently, "and while you are making up your mind hand over that little book you are carrying."

The youth went green.

"Book, sir!" he gasped. "I haven't a book. Oh, you're not the police? For God's sake say you're not the police!"

"I'd scorn to admit it," said Haynes. "Hand over that book."

The youth was speechless. He would have fallen, but one of the detectives caught him by the arm.

"The book," said Haynes shortly.

"I haven't got it." said the young man faintly. "Oh, I've been a fool! I've been a fool!"

"Why say 'have been'?" snarled Haynes. "Hand over that book like a good boy."

"I haven't got it, sir. I gave it to the gentleman last night."

"Last night!"

Haynes knew he spoke the truth.

"To the gentleman in there?" He pointed to the house, and the youth nodded.

"He was going to make arrangements to get me out of the country. That's why I came to see him this morning," blurted Mr Snape.

"Take him away," said Haynes, "and lose him."

Half a dozen strides carried him to the front door of 475. He pressed the hell, and after some little delay the door was opened by a janitor.

"You have a man living here who calls himself Grey," said Haynes.

"Yes, sir," replied the man. "He lives in the first floor flat, flat number 2."

"Is he in now?" asked Haynes.

"He was half an hour ago, sir. He came to the door and asked me if I would stand by to open the street door as soon as I heard a ring. That's why I didn't keep you waiting," grinned the janitor.

"Good," said Haynes, and turned to his henchman. "Hold this door. Let nobody in or out. If it's Sweizer, he is one of the trickiest men in the German service. Whatever attempts to come out, even if it looks like a baby in arms, hold it. It will probably be Sweizer!"

He went up the stairs two at a time and reached the broad landing, from whence two doors opened, one of which bore in neat gold letters the cipher 2.

He pressed a little electric bell-push and heard the faint tinkle within. He waited some time, but there was no answer, and he pressed the bell again. The janitor had followed him up.

"Have you a master key?" asked Haynes.

The man hesitated until Haynes had shown him his warrant card.

The lock turned in the hand of the janitor and scenting trouble he stepped back.

Haynes waited for the door to open wide and walked into the little hall in which an electric light was burning. From the hall gave three doors. The first on the left was a bathroom and empty, the second was a bedroom. Somebody had slept there the night previous, the bed was unmade and a half-consumed glass of whisky and soda stood on a table in the centre of the room. Otherwise it was also empty.

Haynes approached the third room cautiously, flung open the door, and stepped in, revolver in hand, but this also was empty. It was the dining room, handsomely but tastefully furnished. Two long windows looked out into Bloomsbury Place, but of any human inhabitant there was no sign. Two canaries chirped gaily in a cage in front of the window, and Haynes nodded.

Sweizer had one passion—for song-birds—and had more than once escaped betrayal through this eccentricity of his.

Haynes made careful search of the room, and came back to where the janitor was standing.

"Send the man up you see at the door," he said, "but wait, he won't come for you."

He walked out and called his assistant, and together they made a second exploration.

"There's no way out," said Haynes, "not even the fire escape."

He looked through the through the bathroom window, and caught a glimpse of the two watchers who had been posted in the rear of the building. Obviously he could not have gone this way.

"You are sure you saw Mr Grey this morning?"

"I will swear to it," said the janitor earnestly.

Haynes opened every cupboard, peered into every recess which might conceal a man, but without success. Against the wall of the dining-room was a large side-board, the doors of which were locked.

"Open that," said Haynes, "with a poker if you cannot do anything better."

The detective produced a bunch of keys, and his second attempt succeeded in turning the lock, but again he drew blank. The cupboards beneath the sideboard were empty.

"Curiouser and curiouser," said Haynes. "He was in here half an hour ago. There's no way out except by the door. There are no trapdoors in the ceiling, because there is an occupied flat above. And yet undoubtedly he has gone."

His eyes wandered round the room and again rested on the big sideboard. Then something attracted his attention, and he bent down and examined the carpet.

"Looks like the mark of a wheel," he said, "as if something had been rolled over it. Now I come to look," he went on slowly, "that side-board has unusually serviceable castors. Give a hand. We'll pull the side-board into the middle of the room."

There was no necessity, however, to do much more than pull the big bit of furniture a few inches from the wall to discover the mode of retreat. Behind it, cut through the solid wall, was a square opening, 4 ft. by 4 ft.

Haynes jerked the sideboard out, and dashed through the aperture. He found himself in a room which evidently had recently been tenanted.

The detective who followed him gasped.

"This is the house they were taking the piano-case from."

"And in the piano-case was our friend, Mr Sweizer," said Haynes grimly, and in his pocket the I.D. code, which by this time is on its way to Germany; but unless Sweizer is a better man than I he won't accompany the book."

"That's Sweizer's way," said Haynes later. "He had both flats, one adjoining the other, and had prepared his get-away from the first. His confederates waited day and night for the telephoned order to move the piano case. As soon as he found the house was being watched he 'phoned for the furniture removers, passed through the hole he had cut into the furnished flat he had hired next door. He bought the piano a month ago from the owner of the flat—a long headed devil is Sweizer, but I'll match heads with him."

The veritable head of the German Foreign Intelligence Department is Colonel Von Schiff, a stout, bald man, who chews plug tobacco and seldom talks. Major Haynes had met Von Schiff at Algeciras in the year of the great peace conference which brought about the war of 1914, and had been impressed by his simplicity. Von Schiff was no less impressed by Haynes—he was just plain Hiram Haynes in those days—and sought to enlist his services for special work.

This fact Von Schiff remembered with a grunt as he read the closely-written report which had arrived a few hours before, and had come to him from the Wilhemstrasse by the hand of the Under-Minister, who also brought a small grey book in a much-sealed envelope.

That very formal gentleman sat at the opposite side of Von Schiff's big writing-table, and his attitude was deferential, for not only was Von Schiff well born, but he was by reason of his position one of the most powerful men in the Empire.

Herr Von Schiff grunted again, and was unusually loquacious.

"Haynes is a very clever man, Baron. I admire him. I also admire our good friend Sweizer, who seems to me to be in the tightest fix of his life. Only one man in the world can catch him. That man is Haynes. Unless I intervene quickly I lose Sweizer. Better I think the world loses Haynes. Also it is necessary that Sweizer should return to explain the code he has managed to send us."

Von Schiff pressed a bell on his desk, and after a little wait, during which time neither man spoke, the door opened, and a good-looking young officer appeared and saluted.

Von Schiff swung round lazily in his revolving chair.

"Lieutenant Müller," he said, "you are not married, and you have no parents."

"That is true, Herr Colonel."

"You are not affianced either."

The young man hesitated.

"No, Herr Colonel," he said.

"That is good. I will not ask you if you are in love—all healthy young men are in love. You speak English and know England very well?"

"Yes, Herr Colonel."

"Good again. To-morrow you will leave for England via Holland. You will be furnished with an American passport. You will make your way to London and seek out Major Haynes, of the Counter-Espionage Bureau, and you will shoot him dead."

"Yes, Herr Colonel."

"You will probably be hanged," Von Schiff went on calmly, as though he were discussing the possibility of his agent having a rough sea crossing, "but it is for 'König und Vaterland.' That is all."

The young man saluted and went out, closing the door behind him as he went.

Only one piece of advice did Von Schiff tender the next morning when he said good-bye to his subordinate.

"You must shoot quickly or you will die quickly," he said. "Haynes is an admirable trick-shot. And let me give you one more word. Colonel Sweizer, of the Great General Staff, is somewhere in hiding in England. If it is your fortune to establish touch with him you will give him limitless assistance—but you will shoot Haynes."

With a pleasant nod he dismissed his messenger to his death, and went on with the work which the arrival of the young man had interrupted.

A fortnight later an attendant brought a card into the office of Major Haynes, and Haynes glanced at it.

"Mr Herbert Miller," he said. "Oh, yes; that is the man who telegraphed that he had something important to communicate."

There was a gentle knock.

"Come in," said Haynes, and the door opened and admitted a young and quietly-dressed and immensely British-looking young man, who carried a stick and a hat in his right hand.

"Major Haynes?" he asked pleasantly. Haynes did not reply till the door was shut, and then he said with a smile—

"Major Haynes is behind you."

The young man half-turned before he realised the trick. As he swung back to his original position there was a deafening report.

"Sorry," said Haynes. "I'm afraid I have slightly damaged your hat. Don't trouble to pick up your revolver unless you are frightfully anxious to figure in the German casualty list."

The young man was pale. He raised his bleeding hand, and examined it calmly before he returned his gaze to the man at the desk.

"I always shoot a man who comes into this office holding his hat in such a manner as leaves me to suppose that he is hiding a pistol behind it," he said apologetically.

"It is merely a flesh wound," said the visitor coolly.

Haynes deftly bound the damaged hand with a handkerchief.

"I believe there is nothing to be gained by asking you questions, particularly as I know so much." he said. "You are Lieut. Ferdinand Müller, of the 18th Westphalian Regiment, attached to the Intelligence Bureau, and you left Berlin fifteen days ago with instructions to find and shoot me. Those instructions were given to you by my good friend Von Schiff."

The young man did not reply.

"I will not have you executed, nor, indeed, do I intend that you shall be arrested. I am going to send you back to Germany by the way you came, on one condition." Haynes proceeded.

The prisoner, for prisoner he was, eyed him keenly.

"The condition is not a very onerous one," Haynes went on. "I merely ask you to give me your word of honour that when you reach Holland you will notify your chief by telegram that your attempt has failed, and that you will relate to him the circumstances, and that you will not leave Holland until you receive instructions from him."

"When do I go back?" Müller asked.

"You return to-morrow. In the meantime I will ask you to be my guest. Oh, by the way, you might tell your chief that I arrested his good friend Sweizer yesterday."

He glanced keenly at Lieutenant Müller as he spoke, but that young man showed no sign of interest.

Lieutenant Müller left by the morning train, and was escorted to the mail packet by two plain clothes officers, who crossed to the Hook with him, and did not let him out of their sight until he landed on the desolate quay.

One little adventure he had on board. He was sitting in the deck cabin reserved for him when a grimy-looking fireman passed the door. He took little notice, save to wonder why the ship's officers allowed their firemen on deck even on a stormy day when the decks were deserted.

Presently the man came shuffling past again with a big piece of oily waste in his hand. He hesitated at the door, threw a glance left and right, and then apparently catching sight of the detectives moved on, not, however, before he made that queer little gesture with his hand by which the agents of the German Intelligence Service make themselves known to one another.

Lieutenant Müller smiled. The appearance of an agent on a cross-sea packet was not unexpected, but before he could give the answering salute the man had vanished, and was no more seen on the voyage.

From the Hague he sent through the Embassy code the very fullest account of his adventure, omitting nothing save the record of his own indiscretion.

Late in the afternoon he received a telegram prefaced with the word, "Swartz," which means "Urgent and imperative." It was in the code which every officer of the Higher Intelligence Service must memorise as part of his test examination.

It ran:—

"SWEIZER IS AT THE HAGUE. HE CROSSED ON YOUR BOAT. ARRANGE NECESSARY PASSPORTS AND BADGE WITH THE EMBASSY. MEET HIM CORNER OF VYERBERG AT 11, AND GIVE HIM MONEY AND DOCUMENTS. ALSO, FOLLOWING WRITTEN INSTRUCTIONS, SWEIZER MUST TRAVEL FOURTH CLASS THROUGH GERMANY; MUST NOT REVEAL HIMSELF UNTIL HE REACHES BERLIN. HAYNES LEAVES LONDON TO-NIGHT FOR HAGUE. MOST URGENT SWEIZER LEAVES AT ONCE. YOU STAY HAGUE AND WATCH HAYNES. URGENT."

So Haynes had either lied or the elusive Sweizer had made his escape. Thereafter Lieutenant Müller was a busy man.

Sweizer's case was not an unusual one, and both money and credentials reposed in the breast pocket of Lieutenant Müller's coat when he arrived on the deserted Vyerberg that night. He stood for some time outside the Gavangenpoort, that grim prison where John de Witt had met death, then strolled along to the corner of the plaats.

A man came shuffling toward him, a man with bent back and untidy dress. Müller looked at him keenly, and recognised the "fireman" he had seen on the deck of the packet.

As he came to the officer the shambling figure showed his face and put out his hand.

"Quick," he whispered. "I am being followed."

Müller saw the figure of a man pacing slowly toward him in the shadow of the museum building, and slipped a packet into the other's hands.

"Instructions written," he said in a low voice. "I will hold your watcher."

He turned toward the approaching man and heard the feel of the fireman receding behind him.

Müller met the watcher, and squarely blocked his way.

"Why," he said in English, "it is my companion and guardian angel—Mr Something-or-Other, from Scotland Yard."

It was one of the detectives who had accompanied him to Holland, and the man laughed.

"That's right, Mr Müller—just taking a breath of fresh air. Beautiful night, isn't it?" he said, and would have passed on, but Müller detained him.

"Come and drink a glass of schnapps," he said.

"I'm afraid—"

"Nonsense," said Müller, but the detective shook off his detaining hand and strode in pursuit of the man he had been following.

The fireman had disappeared, and Müller went back to his hotel confident that he had disappeared for good.

"At midnight," said Colonel Von Schiff to his first secretary, "I expect a visitor. He may not be presentable, but he is to be shown in to me—and you will remain behind on duty in case you are needed."

"Yes, Herr Colonel," replied the official, and went out full of bitter wishes for the Herr Colonel's future, for midnight visitors (and they were many) were the bane of the secretary's life.

Schiff pulled a telephone to him and called an official of the Kriegsministerium.

"S. is back," he said, "he arrives tonight—it may be necessary to work all night on the code, and in this case I shall need two experts who are on the telephone. I may not want them, but they must be ready to come if I call them."

He hung up the receiver and went to his frugal dinner.

At five minutes to twelve he sat at his desk turning the pages of a certain grey code book under the light of the electric desk lamp.

At midnight exactly there was a tap at the door, and his secretary entered.

"A person to see you, Herr Colonel—he gives the word 'Swartz.'"

"Show him in."

The secretary came back with the visitor.

"Shut the door and go," said Von Schiff.

The door clicked, and the colonel turned with a smile.

"Well, Sweizer, this is an unexpected pleasure. You haven't been in Berlin for five years."

"Three to be exact," said the newcomer. As he spoke he moved towards the desk, and at his last word his hand shot out and wrenched the grey book from Schiff's grasp.

Von Schiff leapt to his feet, peering through the half-gloom, for the shaded table lamp was the only light in the room.

"Speak in a conversational tone and preferably in English, Heinrich," said the visitor.

Von Schiff stared from the uncleanly face of the man to the stout black muzzle of the Browning which the visitor held.

"Gott im Himmel!" he gasped. "Haynes!"

"S-sh!" warned Haynes. "Sit down. You know me, dear lad. I never broke a promise. When I say I'll shoot—"

"I don't doubt it," said Von Schiff coolly as he sank back into his chair. "Well, I have always admired you. You are immense. I ought to have expected this. I suppose the code telegram I had from Sweizer at The Hague—"

"Was from me," said Haynes. "Von Müller was quite useful in his way. He's quite a good boy. By-the-bye you ought to make a good intelligence officer out of him."

"Have a cigar," said Von Schiff, his hand on the knob of a drawer.

"I'd sooner be shot than poisoned," confessed Haynes. "Take your hand away from that drawer, brother, or you'll be sleuthing round Heaven to-night."

Von Schiff picked up his own cigar from the edge of the desk and drew it alight. Then he chuckled.

"Very good—most excellent," he said, with genuine admiration. "How are you going to get away?"

"Motor car at the door. Aeroplane rendezvous at umpteen minutes past ump, and ho for Bonnie England!"

"But, seriously—"

"Well, I'll tell you—in the Embassy bag of the Chinese Ambassador, camouflaged as a registered letter."

Von Schiff puffed at his cigar. "I'll tell you how you're going, if you're wise," he said. "You're going the way you came. Sweizer, by the way, is arrested, of course?"

Haynes nodded.

"You shall have your life for his. Give me your word—"

"Give nothing," said Haynes, and backed to the door.

Three days later a German Staff officer approached a sentry on the Dutch frontier, and the sentry presented arms.

"What are your orders?" barked the officer.

"To allow no person to approach the frontier line. Herr General Staff Officer," bellowed the Landsturm soldier.

"Go on, pig. What else?"

"To shoot at sight any prisoner of war who attempts to cross the frontier line."

"Hurry, hurry, thickhead! What else, numbskull?"

"To watch for a civilian, tall and thin-faced."

"Ah, at last, fool!" cried the officer. "You should have told me that at first. Which is the frontier line?"

"That white path, Herr General Staff Officer."

The officer walked forward, looking about him curiously.

"Have you seen anybody escape from Germany?" he called back.

"No, illustrious Herr."

"Then watch me," said Haynes as he crossed the frontier.

CHAPTER IX

THE DISAPPEARANCE OF LADY MARY BRETLEY

Lady Mary Bretley, the daughter of His Majesty's Secretary of State for Crown Colonies, left her home at ten o'clock on the morning of May 29 with the intention of attending a meeting of the St Anne's Red Cross Comforts Committee, of which she was a member.

One of the prettiest and most popular girls in London society, a fearless rider to hounds, and an amateur tennis champion, she had that mens sana which proverbially accompanies the corpore sano. In other words, she was a singularly intelligent, clear-headed girl without a fad, and because of her work on the Committee of the Charity Organisation Society, without many illusions.

She left her father's house in Downing Street, and was seen by the police sergeant on point duty at two minutes after the hour. She turned up Whitehall and walked to Trafalgar Square Underground Station, apparently with the intention of travelling by "tube" to Regent's Park, the committee holding its meeting at Lady Grimboro's house in Portland Place.

She was seen by the elevator attendant, who recognised her, and was seen also by a conductor, a youth named Bodden, who saw her in conversation with two men who sat one on each side of her. The three were talking very earnestly, and Bodden heard Lady Mary say—"I can get the money if you can—"

The three left the station at Paddington, which was four stations beyond where Lady Mary had arranged to alight, for the attendant on the escalator remembered one of the men pay excess fare for three.

From that moment all trace was lost of her. That she did not return home for lunch did not alarm her father, for it was usual for the girl to lunch out. She was due at four o'clock to accompany her father to the opening of an exhibition of war pictures, and though he was naturally troubled by her non-appearance he was not seriously alarmed.

When she did not return for dinner he communicated with another member of St Annes Committee, and then learnt for the first time that his daughter had not attended the meeting. Seriously perturbed by now, he communicated with the police, the hospitals were questioned, and three of Scotland Yard's best sleuths got on the track of the missing girl, and traced her to Paddington.

The descriptions of the two men circulated to all police stations were:—

1. Man of 35, dark brown beard, clipped short; fair complexion, tall (about 6 ft.); wore a fawn dustcoat and grey Stetson hat.

2. Man of 25. Dark, small black moustache, good complexion; dressed in grey tweed suit, Derby hat, enamelled leather button boots.

Both men looked as though they were recovering from a long illness—all the witnesses agreed as to this. Lord Bretley, the Minister, was distracted with anxiety. The war had hit him hard enough already. One of his sons had been killed on the Somme, one had been taken prisoner at Loos, and, according to the accounts which were reaching England through code messages and from repatriated prisoners, he had had a particularly bad time.

To add to his misfortune, his youngest and favourite son—favourite in the same manner and for the same reason that most younger sons are favoured—had been reported missing since the third battle of Passchendale. On top of these calamities came what seemed the greatest of all.

Throughout the night search continued, and in the morning came a further item of news. The girl had been seen at Paddington at 10.35. At two o'clock that afternoon she had been seen by the branch manager of the London Guarantee Trust Banking Corporation. She had walked into the Clunie Street office of the bank, and had drawn out £600 from her private account.

The manager who saw her jokingly said that he hoped she would not be robbed, and she had made no reply except to ask whether he could tell her the rates of exchange on the principal neutral cities.

He saw her join two men who were waiting in a cab outside and drive away. The taxi driver, who was traced, stated that whilst the lady was in the bank the men talked together in a foreign tongue, which he believed was German because of the "ja's" and "neins," and other words he recognised because he had at one time been in private service with a German family.

The distracted father sought his colleague, the Minister for Internal Affairs.

"The best thing you can do is to call in Haynes," said that official. "This may be a political rather than a criminal job."

So they brought Haynes from his pleasant club and put all the facts before him.

Lord Bretley was a man of sixty, tall, straight, and austere. His severity of countenance and a certain coldness in his manner did not make for popularity, but his peculiar views on international law, his known objection to reprisals, and his undisguised contempt for "the criticisms of demagogues" had not exactly endeared him to the people.

When Haynes arrived he was pacing his study, pausing to throw a word to his fellow Minister, who rose to greet Haynes as he was announced.

"Here is Major Haynes, Lord Bretley," said the Minister of the Interior, and his Lordship swung round and favoured the newcomer with a cold stare.

"I don't know that this is a matter for your department," he said grudgingly.

His antipathy to anything associated with the military was known to Haynes, and he smiled.

"My department isn't frantically anxious to touch the case," he said calmly, "if the case in question is the disappearance of Lady Mary, as I presume it is."

Bretley glowered at him. Opposition he hated, and he recognised opposition here.

"I don't like your tone, Major Haynes," he began, but Haynes interrupted him.

"Before we go any farther, Lord Bretley, let us understand one another," he said. "If you want me to take up these investigations you must disabuse your mind of the illusion that you are superior clay because you are a Minister or a Peer of the realm, or what-not. I just don't care tuppence whether you are a Marquis, a Duke, or a dustman, Prime Minister of England, or Bill Jones. I have just come from the execution of a gentleman whose ancestral records go back to the Ice Age in B.C. six million."

Lord Bretley's stare this time held somewhat reluctant amusement.

"Go ahead then," he said gruffly. "Carstairs will tell you all that has happened."

"Mr Carstairs has told me the main story," said Haynes. "Has anything fresh happened?"

Lord Bretley walked to his desk, and picking up a sheet of paper handed it to Haynes.

It was a note written in pencil on the back of a handbill announcing changes of time in the running of certain trains.

"Dear Daddy" (it began), "please, please don't worry about me. I shall be away for a fortnight.—Mary."

"Is that all?"

"No. Something else has happened. My daughter was in this house last night."

"Here?"

"Here. She must have come in between two and three after I was in bed. She was accompanied by one or both of the men. My safe was opened, and three passport blanks were extracted."

"Ordinary passports?"

"No. The yellow passport which is used in case of emergency when we wish to send someone abroad in a hurry and there is no time to photograph him. One was filled in in my daughter's name, one in the name of Henry Smith, and another in the name of Walter or William Jones."

Haynes nodded.

"I see—they left the impressions on the blotting pad—anything else?"

"The passports were sealed with my official seal and signed by my daughter, whose writing is so like mine that I myself find it difficult to distinguish between the two hands."

Haynes stroked his chin thoughtfully.

"What is the police theory?"

"That she has acted under compulsion. Two Germans, who for some reason or other wish to leave the country, have by threat or by the exercise of some other influence induced my daughter to assist them."

"Have you received any news from the ports?"

"Yes. Three people answering to the description of the two men and my daughter left Folkestone for Boulogne early this morning and landed in France. They must have motored through the night. We are now trying to secure some trace of them beyond Boulogne."

Haynes asked a few more questions and then left.

The wires were busy all that day and night. London spoke to Paris and Paris to Marseilles, Pontarlier and Andemasse and Hendage—for all who leave France must go through one or the other of these places.

There were clues enough but none which placed Lady Mary into the hands of her friends, and for ten days the trackers of two secret services pursued their vain inquiries. To add to Lord Bretley's distress, on the following day when he called up Haynes on the 'phone he discovered that that gentleman had vanished too.

Haynes was back in London after a week's absence, but if he saw anything of Mary Bretley he did not speak of her until Doctor Gwinner forced his hand.

Haynes has been criticised for his silence. It has been urged against him that the very thought of a heartbroken father fretting himself to death over the mysterious disappearance of his daughter should have induced him at any rate to put his suspicions into words, but Haynes was a law unto himself, and he had a grievance against his lordship. How far he would have allowed his grievance to carry him it is impossible to say. After Doctor Gwinner's arrival there was no longer any need for mystery.

On that momentous day a man came out through the booking-hall of Charing Cross station and passed on to the pavement, looking about him as though he were in search of an expected friend. He was a tall man, with a fair, trim beard, and he was dressed well though unobtrusively.

He put down the valise he was carrying, and drew a cigar from his waistcoat pocket. He was in the act of lighting this when a hand fell upon his arm, and he turned to see the smiling face of a stranger.

"I'm afraid you've made a mistake," he said pleasantly.

"Not at all," said the stranger. "I am Inspector Burbery, of the Counter-Intelligence Service, and I must ask you to accompany me to the chief of my department."

The fair man shrugged his shoulders and yielded.

"C'est la guerre," he said indifferently. "Will you call a cab or shall I?"

"The cab is here," said the inspector as a taxi moved out of the rank and drew to the kerb. "Let me take your bag."

Five minutes later he was ushered into a very plain office, where a keen-faced officer sat behind a table reading a newspaper.

"Put a chair for Herr Gwinner, Inspector," said Major Haynes cheerfully, "and then I think you can leave us—no, stay."

He beckoned the Inspector back.

"To save all sorts of unpleasantness, will you take Herr Gwinner's pistol from him?"

"My dear sir," protested the visitor, "I assure you—"

"Strapped under his left armpit, but protruding through the arm hole."

"Hold up your arms, please," said the Inspector, and slid his hand under the other's arm, withdrawing it holding a serviceable-looking Browning.

"You need not have been afraid," smiled the imperturbable visitor. "I should not have used it."

"That I know," said Haynes, "and I wasn't afraid for myself. I should have shot you dead before you could have touched it, but the War Office do not like us to kill spies on the premises. It gets the place a bad name. Thank you. You needn't wait, Inspector."

When the door had shut the man laughed again.

"You evidently mistake me for somebody else. My name is Vanderberg, and I am Dutch. I have arrived in London to conduct—"

"Negotiations with the River Plate Export Company," finished Haynes.

"I have letters from—"

"The British Consul at Rotterdam—yes, yes, I know all about that, my dear Herr Gwinner," said Haynes, yawning. "Don't be silly. Your name is Gwinner. You arrived in Holland from Germany on the 17th by the train which reaches the Maas Station, Rotterdam, via Utrecht and Amsterdam. You stayed at the Hotel Leygraaff, where one of my men saw you arrange your little gun for quick and dirty work. You dined on the night of your arrival at the Café Restaurant du Passage on Koorte Hoogstraat, where you met a man from the German Embassy who gave you forged letters of introduction and instructions to get into touch with the chief agent on this side."

Gwinner was no longer smiling. His cigar had gone cold, and though he did not change colour two deep lines showed beneath his eyes.

"Suppose all this is true," he said quietly, "you at least cannot charge me with any specific act of espionage. I am a lawyer, sir, and I know that it is no crime to penetrate into an enemy country."

"Up to a point you're right," nodded Haynes. "Light your cigar—I'm going to be pleasant."

The hand that took the match which Haynes extended trembled ever so slightly, despite all the owner's self-control.

"You see, Herr Doktor—I'm sorry I omitted your title before—I happen to know a great deal about you. You are a Doctor of Law in the University of Bonn. You have got into very serious trouble over money affairs, so that although you were exempted from active service you volunteered to get away from Bonn. You were taken into the Intelligence Bureau at Headquarters because of your knowledge of English, and for that reason were sent to the United Kingdom on a most difficult and dangerous errand."

He paused, but his prisoner made no reply. Haynes had a trick of inviting a reply and at the same time, by the very choice of the moment of pause, catching his vis-a-vis unprepared for an answer.

"The nature of that 'difficult and dangerous' errand I have yet to discover," Haynes went on. "You see I am being frank with you. My representative who shadowed you through Holland knows only this, that the words employed by the Embassy official who gave you your documents were, 'You will remember, Herr Doctor, that your mission is difficult and dangerous.'"

"I see," said the Herr Doctor. He looked at and through Haynes.

"Suppose I tell you that I do not know the nature of my mission—suppose I admit that I am an agent of the German Government, and tell you that I am here in England to discover a German who disappeared from Ingolstadt a little over a week ago, and who is now in England."

He leant back in his chair and laughed softly. He was a Saxon, and a Saxon is the only kind of German that has a sense of humour.

"Believe it or not as you wish, this is the story—The man I am seeking is Reserve Captain Geissler, a very unimportant person until a few days ago. He might have passed through the war the pride of his family but unknown in the larger army circles. Frankly, he was or is not what you would call a gentleman, certainly not—well, you know the German officer of reserve. Until ten days ago he was commandant of Camp 86 at Ingolstadt—a strafe camp to which officer prisoners of war are sent who cause the authorities trouble. They are mainly British officers, and the discipline is strict. I have reason to know that Geissler treated the British badly, and that he had even struck a British officer. He would have been tried by Court-Martial but for the fact that the only witness against him, the victim of his blow, escaped from captivity. Last Friday week Geissler went on leave to visit his parents, who live in a little town on Lake Constance. On the Saturday morning he went out on to the lake in a rowing boat. The lake, as you know, is very carefully patrolled by motor boats, because the opposite shore is Swiss and we have had numerous desertions by this route.

"Geissler was seen by the guard boats paddling aimlessly about near the border 'line'—that is to say, the imaginary line across the lake which represents the German frontier. The morning was misty but not foggy, though the mist was thick enough to hide the Swiss shore. Outside the German line was a motor boat of a powerful make and flying no flag or burgee. The German patrol watching Geissler saw his boat suddenly jerk forward and dart without propulsion toward the frontier line. At the same time the strange motor boat began moving swiftly toward the Swiss shore. What had happened was that somebody had swum from the motor craft to Geissler's boat, fastened a light line to the bow, and Geissler was being towed away—the patrol saw the swimmer clinging to the stern of Geissler's canoe. They fired at both boats, but they disappeared.

"Five days later a certain Legation in London which is not unfriendly to Germany received a telephone call. One of the secretaries answered the 'phone and a voice said hurriedly, speaking in German. 'Inform Berlin that Captain Geissler—' Then something was said which the secretary could not understand, except one word—'Bretley.'"

Haynes touched a bell.

"I am sending you to close arrest until I verify as much of your story as it is possible to confirm. Technically you are a spy, of course, and you may or you may not be brought to trial on that charge."

He drove straight away to Lord Bretley's house, and found the Minister at home.

"I have just sent a messenger for you, sir," said the servant who opened the door. "His Lordship is in the library."

Lord Bretley turned sharply as Haynes entered the room, and came toward him with a beaming face.

"Splendid news, Major," he said, offering both his hands impulsively. "My daughter is in England and safe. And even better than that—you'll never guess!"

"I think I can," said Haynes quietly. "You have two sons, one of whom was a prisoner, the other reported missing. Both, in point of fact, were prisoners, and both have escaped."

Lord Bretley stared at him.

"How do you know?" he asked.

"I guess," said Haynes. "Tell me this. Have you ever had a German in your employ named Geissler?"

"Why, yes," replied the Minister. "A young music master, he taught my daughter, and was soundly thrashed by one of my boys for—well, the infernal rascal made violent love to my daughter."

Haynes smiled and sighed.

"So that was it! By the way, your children are not in London now, of course?"

Again Lord Bretley stared.

"But two of them are coming to see you," Haynes went on, "and the third will come a week later after one of the two have gone away."

"My dear fellow!" exploded Lord Bretley, with a show of his old irritation, "please don't mystify me. What do you know? All you say is true; here is the letter I had from my daughter this morning."

He took up a note from the table and road:—

"Dear Daddy,—Bobby and Jack have escaped from Germany. We are at Moor Keep—"

"Moor Keep?" repeated Haynes, "where is that?"

"It is an old estate of mine in Devonshire—a wild bit of moorland and patched up manor house which I've never used. Why they should go there, Heaven knows."

"Go on, sir," said Haynes.

"I shall bring Bobby to town in two or three days, and Jack will come up next week to report to the War Office. They won't be able to be in town at the same time, for reasons which we will explain later."

He looked at Haynes, and Haynes was laughing.

"Just tell me where I can find Moor Keep, sir," he said, "and I promise you that your family shall all come to London together."

Moor Keep lies on the desolate side of Princetown, due west to the Tavistock road. It sits in a fold of the ragged hills, and is half encircled by a foaming tributary of the Dart. A grim house of undressed stone, half hidden by a clump of trees, it presented a particularly uninviting appearance in the light of a waning moon.

So Haynes thought as he scaled the high wall which surrounds this hunting box of the Bretleys—the last Bretley to follow the Devonshire stag-hounds had been dead for thirty years.

The house was dark and lifeless, and Haynes made his way to the weather-stained front door and knocked.

There was no answer, and he knocked again. He waited a while, and his stick was raised for the third time when the door was opened suddenly.

He looked into the dark hall and guessed rather than saw the tall shadowy figure.

"Who is that?" demanded a voice.

Haynes' sense of fun overcame his discretion, and he replied in German—

"Is the well-born Professor Geissler within?"

"Come in," said the man in the same language.

Haynes stepped across the threshold and found himself gripped by two pairs of arms. A sack was thrown over his head, and he was thrown to the ground. He struggled for a moment, but, realising the futility of resistance, he became passive in the hands of his captors.

"Is the well-born Professor Geissler here?" mocked a voice.

"Yes, he is here, you blighter! I told you, Bobby, they'd send one of their agents looking for the devil."

"What shall we do with him?" asked another voice; but before the answer could come a third voice spoke, evidently from the upper part of the house, and the voice was that of a woman.

"It's all right, Mary," said the man addressed as Bobby. "It's only another Hun—we'll put him in with Geissler."

Haynes was pushed violently down a long passage and through a door which opened on to a flight of stone steps evidently leading to the cellars.

Another door was opened, Haynes was jerked through, and the door clanged behind him. He was in an underground kitchen illuminated by a hanging lamp, and he was not alone.

Sitting at the table, a disconsolate figure, was a German officer, who glared up at the new arrival.

"Untie this rope," said Haynes in German. "I want a little chat with you."

An hour later the tall, bearded young man who was called Bobby brought him food.

"Put it on the table, Captain Bretley," said Haynes in English, and closed the note-book in which he had been writing. "I have all the information I want, and now I think we had better talk this matter over in private."

"Who are you?" asked the astonished young man.

Haynes handed him a badge.

"Intelligence—good Lor'!" gasped the gaoler. "I say, there'll be an awful row about this, won't there?"

"That depends," said Haynes.

Later he sat in the cosy library of Moor Keep in company with two chastened young soldiers and a laughing bright-eyed girl.

"You seem to know most of the story," said Captain Bobby Bretley; "but you don't know it all. Geissler had been a secret service agent in England, and he had a big pull. When Jack was taken prisoner it was Geissler who suppressed his name from the list of prisoners taken—he was in the record office at Berlin at the time. It was Geissler who transferred us to Ingolstadt after getting command of the camp. He gave us a hell of a time. He kept me in cells for three months, he destroyed the letters I wrote home and the letters that came to me. Jack was treated even worse, for Jack had thrashed him. Once or twice he gave us chances to escape, but we knew that he had a platoon waiting to shoot us down if we ever attempted to get away.

"Then one day our chance came. Some of the fellows had dug a tunnel, and they asked us to go with them. Jack and I got away, and made for the Swiss border. I won't describe the perfectly awful time we had—but we got clear. Of course, we should have reported straight away to the nearest British Consul, but Jack and I had laid our plans. I won't tell you how we wangled our way to England—but we did. We told Mary what our scheme was, and she got the money and the passports.

"What was the scheme? To kidnap Geissler, get him to England, and give him some of the medicine he gave to us. Major Haynes, that man is a devil! It wasn't what he did to Jack and me—it was the villainy he practised on the other helpless prisoners of war. He could do it with impunity, because Camp 86 was reserved for the worst characters, chaps like myself who had tried to escape or cheeked German officials. We came to England and laid wait for Mary. We knew that if father got wind of our plan he'd stop it. That's why we come, so to speak, incognito.

"Mary fell in with our scheme like a brick. She got the currency and the passports and we crossed over— we reached Switzerland via Chamonix by-the-way. We meant to get Geissler. You see, we knew that he was going on leave and where he was going. Well, to cut a long story short we reached Constance, hired a launch and went out in search of Geissler. Jack was the swimmer, Mary ran the engine, I was G.O.C. Operations."

He laughed quietly.

"We had good luck. The first day we caught him, smuggled him through Switzerland and France. We couldn't have done it but for the help we got from a man we never saw. It sounds extraordinary but it is a fact. Wherever we went we had a note from him—just a few words signed with the initial letter 'M'. It was he who told us that the Swiss police were searching for us at Berne. He told us how to get across the frontier and gave us a sealed envelope to give to the frontier guard and another for the officials on the boat at Bordeaux. It was he who gave us a note which passed us at Penzance. He seemed to flutter round us all the time and yet we never saw him."

Lady Mary Bretley's gaze was fixed on Haynes and she saw the twinkle in his eyes.

"Why!" she cried suddenly, "I know—it was you!"

Bobby gaped at him.

"You!" he said, "but what did the 'M' stand for?"

"Me!" said Haynes.

CHAPTER X

TEN DIVISIONS AND A RED-HAIRED GIRL

There were people who liked Major Haynes; there were others who disliked him intensely. No small proportion of the latter lie in a certain little burying ground not many miles from the Tower Moat.

It is related of Bjornken that when he was asked on the chilly morning they led him to the chair before the firing party if there was anything they could do for him he answered:

"Tell me that Haynes has broken his neck—it will cheer me up."

But then Bjornken had a sense of humour.

Colonel Carsland was denied this quality and to this day, sitting in the cold shades of a compulsory retirement, he sees nothing funny in the episode of the Red Haired Chorus Girls and refers to Haynes as "no gentleman" which is feeble when compared with Bjornken's little joke.

"I must confess," said the Director of Counter-Intelligence, "that Haynes gets me rattled."

His chief of staff sniffed.

"For God's sake don't sniff," said General Marriness irritably, "you don't like Haynes, Colonel. His methods aren't the methods we are used to—but we're fighting a new kind of war and dealing with a new kind of enemy. Over in the Military Intelligence Department they'd jump at him if we gave him his marching orders. I confess that I like him—he is the sort of man I'd have given my skin for when I was doing police work in India."

The austere colonel fingered his trim white moustache.

"There is limit to everything, sir. One doesn't expect a C.E. man to live a wholly conventional life and one isn't too exacting as to the—er—morals of young officers, but from a man of Major Haynes' position of responsibility one expects—well a certain show of decency and all that sort of thing. The Duchess of Barside was saying—"

"Dam' the Duchess of Barside," growled the old man, "an interfering old fool who paints her face."

"The Duchess is a personal friend of mine," said the other stiffly as he rose.

"Sit down—sit down, Carsland," said the general testily, "we've known each other too long to quarrel—we'll have Haynes in and put it to him. He'll rattle me. He always rattles me," he pressed a bell, "I never rag him but I've always visions of him pulling a gun and holding me up till I've apologised—oh, sergeant, tell Major Haynes I want him."

When the non-commissioned, officer had gone the general swung round in his chair, his shaggy brows drawn together in a frown, his blue eyes gloomy with doubt. Major General Marriness, in his time the most efficient police chief that India had ever known had little sympathy with the views of straight-laced leaders of Purity Leagues, even when they were entitled to four bars of ermine on their robes of state. He was all the more embarrassed, if the truth be known, that his assistant, appointed by himself for old friendship's sake, had not been content to sit tight and play a passive role in the direction of the affairs of the department but had plunged into the task of management of affairs which he imperfectly understood with all the misguided dogmatism which the military mind brings to problems of administration.

Therefore the secret uneasiness of Old Man Marriness; therefore his agonies of doubt; therefore, too, a doubling of his labour and vigilance.

The door opened and Major Haynes came in and saluted.

"Shut the door," mumbled the general, "sit down Haynes. Now then—er—um. There's a matter I want to discuss with you... very delicate, Haynes..."

He looked anxiously at his second.

"Affecting the prestige and standing of the department," said Colonel Carsland in an evenness of tone which was in itself a menace.

"Yes sir?" said Haynes innocently, "have I been misbehaving again?"

"Chorus girls, my boy," growled the general, "red-haired chorus girls—dash it all Haynes. You can't do it, my boy! Supper parties with red haired chorus girls—what the devil do you mean by it—hey?"

Haynes smiled.

"Oh that," he said in a tone of relief, "I thought it was something serious."

"It is serious Major," snapped the colonel, "your conduct is the talk of London. My friend the Duchess of Barside" (the general groaned) "who does a great deal of useful social work amongst these girls tells me that your—your absurd preference for red-haired chorus girls is—is becoming a public scandal sir. There isn't a theatrical dressing room in London, sir, that doesn't know that a red-haired chit of a girl has only to crook her finger to have you dancing round her. You had a dozen of them at Cockham one week end to stay with you—"

"And my highly respectable aunt," murmured Haynes.

"Yes, I admit they were chaperoned, but is that the reputation we wish our department to bear? You'll have questions asked in parliament about it, sir. Why sir, even my girl's governess, a charming young lady living a sheltered life—er—wanted to know if her hair was the colour—"

"Is she red too?" asked Haynes eagerly. "Oh, splendid! I'll tell you the kind I like—red with a deep touch of bronze so that in the sunlight it looks—"

"I really am not interested in your strange tastes," said the exasperated Assistant Director, "what I am concerned about—and what I must insist upon—"

"We will come to that," interrupted the general quietly. "I think the best thing I can do, if you will excuse me, Carsland, is to see Major Haynes alone."

Reluctantly the colonel withdrew.

"Bolt the door boy," growled Marriness, and when his visitor had obeyed:

"Have a cigar—now, what's the game?"

"The game sir?"

The old man nodded.

"Don't hand me any of that innocent child stuff," he said. "Chorus girls aren't in your line, Haynes. I know something about men and you're not that kind of man."

Haynes hesitated.

"Well?"

"Well sir," he hesitated again, "I'm going to ask something you won't like."

The general smiled.

"Go ahead—I'll brace myself."

"This is unofficial between man and man." The general nodded and winced a little for he knew what was coming, "Then sir, I ask you this—if I tell you will you regard my information as confidential as between ourselves?"

"In other words, it is not to be an office matter," said the General slowly, "or, not to put too fine a point on it, Colonel Carsland must not be told!"

Haynes nodded.

"H'm."

Loyalty to his friend, an appreciation of that friend's inefficiency and a greater loyalty to The Cause were all comprehended in General Marriness's grunt.

"Go ahead."

Haynes nodded again.

"You may have heard of Rosa Stahl? You'11 find a brief reference to her in the von Dnieper dossier, and she was mentioned by one of the witnesses—Harbeit, the fellow who turned states' evidence at the trial of Bjornken."

"I remember—she was the agent in South America who financed von Dnieper, yes?"

"I believe that she is one of the most dangerous women in the German service," said Haynes and added abruptly: "and she is in England."

"Where?"

"Heaven knows. All that I know is that she is in England. The Boche always works his big stunts with a woman—that was why I was so happy to see the last of the Princess Sabochiffski—and there is something big afoot for him to risk Rosa. She is the biggest thing they've had in South America. Clever, resourceful and brought up to the game—her father was the Kaiser's Press Agent till the Princes Trust Swindle drove him to the Argentine."

"I still don't understand—I suppose you've circulated a description of the lady?"

"There is no description."

"Her photograph?"

"There is no photograph—that's the trouble. There aren't a dozen people in the world who have seen her without a veil and those few are Germans. Old Stahl kept his household as exclusive as a Moorish bashah. I saw her once at Rio driving. A black gown and a mantilla. I didn't take much notice of her. After the Bjornken trial I ordered photographs of her but though we employed the cutest press photographer in New York City he could never manoeuvre a picture."

"What else do you know of her?"

Haynes drew a breath.

"She's clever, can sing in five languages, can dance beautifully, is fond of theatres—and—"

"And—?"

"She has red hair."

There was a silence.

"I see—you think you'll attract her to you?"

Major Haynes smiled.

"It is possible—if my infamy is sufficiently well advertised."

The general played with the office ruler.

"Why should not Colonel Carsland know all this?" he asked.

"Not on your life sir," said Haynes vigorously. "I've all sorts of respect for the colonel, for a gallant and able slayer of Afridis, Tigers and time, but—"

"One word more before you go," said the general as Haynes stood by the door. "What is this woman's stunt?"

"Anything big—reserves, anti-submarine measures, new aeroplane types, they're too small for her. She's on the strategical side—chit-chat of the War Cabinet, new policies—unity of command, that is more in her line. Or something bigger."

On his way back to his zoom he passed under the review of the colonel's disapproving eye.

"Insolent cub," muttered the colonel.

"Rum old devil," thought Haynes.

That night he gave a party at the Clifton Galleries which will be remembered in theatre-land for many moons. It was that stand-up-supper-dance which moved the writer of "What People Ask" in the pages of London Gossip to demand breathlessly:

Who is the gay major who gave a Ginger Party at the Clifton the other night?

Isn't Whitehall a little horrified at the Indiscretions of a member of the Intelligence Bureau?

Is this an ideal method for winning the war?

We wonder what the Tommies in the trenches think about it all?"

It was Major Haynes' famous Auburn Hop, and the Ragtime Coon Band was weary enough before the last visitor left.

News came to Whitehall before the frenzied queries of London Gossip oozed from their writer's pen.

"Disgraceful... my dear fellow!... this is beyond all reason! I say... really...."

Indignation made Colonel Carsland incoherent.

"Ah yes," said his chief mildly, "boys will be boys—hey! Too bad—too bad!"

"It is infamous—after what you told him yesterday general!"

The general went a guilty red.

"Yes, yes, of course—I must speak to Haynes."

"The Duchess said—" began the colonel.

"A-B-C-D-E-F-G-H." said the general rapidly. It was a system of his own dedicated to a wife long since dead who had suggested this harmless substitution for the lurid expletives of her lord, "oh my dear man—oh my blessed friend, do leave the duchess out of it. Now listen."

He fell back into the chair and brought his fist down upon the desk with one motion and when he spoke it was less the voice of a dear old friend than the official voice of Major General Sir John Marriness, K.C.B., Director-General of Counter-Intelligence.

"Haynes is doing departmental work in his own way—he has my authority and sanction for any Bacchanalian excess in which he chooses to indulge—"

"But—"

"Please let me finish. It is my earnest desire that you should cease to trouble your head about Haynes— let him go his own way."

"Very good sir," said the colonel in a tone which said plainly "Very bad."

The Director met Haynes on his way to lunch.

"Any luck?" he asked.

"It depends on what you call luck," said the other cautiously. "Look here, sir, would your reputation survive lunch with a chorus girl—if I were present to lend an air of respectability to an otherwise degrading spectacle?"

"My reputation has survived intimate association with some of the dandiest political assassins that India has produced," said Sir John grimly. "Produce your lunch and your chorus girl—a red-haired one?"

"Very red-haired," said Haynes gravely, and then: "by-the-way, she will ask me if I knew Ostend before the war and will tell me she knows every yard of the town."

The general stared at him.

"What makes you think that—has she spoken of it before?"

Haynes shook his head smilingly.

"I've never spoken to her for more than five minutes," he said.

At a little restaurant in Dean Street and in a corner of the room, screened from the gaze of the vulgar by a bead curtain, they found their guest.

She was undeniably pretty, her hair exceptionally beautiful and she flashed a smile at her host and his companion, and did not seem in any way disconcerted by the arrival of a third guest.

"I hope I'm not intruding," said Sir John.

"Not a bit," laughed the girl. "I'm the intruder—didn't you think it was awfully bold of me to invite myself to lunch after only knowing you for two minutes?" she addressed Haynes.

"I thought it was wonderful of you," said Haynes ecstatically.

("You can never go wrong in describing anything as 'wonderful' that relates to the life of the chorus," he explained after.)

She looked at him with amusement as he ordered the lunch.

"You're awfully keen on red-haired girls aren't you?" she asked later.

"Keen is not the word—I am perfectly potty!" he raved—even Sir John winced at the vulgarity.

The conversation continued at this high intellectual level throughout the meal.

Once she said she adored military men and Haynes asked her pointed questions about her "boy," whereat she laughed the louder.

Then (it was nearly at the close of the meal) she asked carelessly:

"Do you know Ostend?"

"A little—do you?"

"Like a book—lord, I shall be glad when the war's over. I used to go there every summer—stayed at Westende at the Littoral—a jolly nice hotel on the Digue du Mer—forty minutes run from Ostend."

"Cars every hour," suggested Haynes.

"Every twenty minutes," she corrected. "What a lovely beach, miles of it at low tide—I suppose the Germans are there now. Why don't we go and turn them out?"

"I wonder?" said Haynes politely.

Soon after they left the restaurant and the girl went to her flat. She was not playing in London she said—she had just finished a tour in the provinces and was "resting". Would she see him again? Haynes said that it was likely.

The two men drove back to the office.

"Well, is that your Rosa Stahl?" asked the general.

"What do you think—did you notice anything?"

"Many things—she is well, even extravagantly dressed and has jewels."

"All new," nodded Haynes. "Even the rings—you can tell new jewellery—it has a hard look. The furs were new, so were the shoes and the costume."

"She speaks English well enough."

"With a slight Cockney accent—which might be acquired from a bad teacher. That proves nothing. But she understands such colloquialisms as 'potty'—I saw you jump, sir—which means that she's genuine. Did you notice I asked her how she spent her Sundays and how naturally she answered 'in the train'—that's the lot of the touring company."

"But what about Ostend—how did you know she would ask—"

Haynes smiled cryptically.

He had an assistant, one Dane, a youth of great, seriousness of mind, and he found him on his return to the office conscientiously struggling with the singularly uninteresting dossier of a Belgian who had come into conflict with the authorities over a prosaic matter of registration. It was one of those cases which delight the official mind. The Belgian was born at Malmedy which is Belgian on one side of the street and German on the other, and one particular building is Belgium in the parlour and Germany in the kitchen. The unfortunate man in question had been born in this building.

"What the dickens are you digging out?" demanded Haynes.

"Colonel Carsland wants more data about this man Kloots—the colonel has seen a Belgian doctor from Malmedy who can swear that Kloots was born in the kitchen, which was also the living room of the Kloots family. Here is the colonel's memorandum."

He handed a thick sheet of note-paper heavily embossed with a coat of arms and 'Pingley Manor, Basingstoke', and read the scribbled notes of the colonel's requirements from "1. Copy of Certificate of Jan Kloots' birth" to "Plan of Malmedy prefaced by R.E. Survey."

"It la certainly weird the amount of joy the office men get out of this sort of thing," he said. He looked at the memo again. "The colonel spends a lot of money on his stationery," he noted mechanically.

He lunched again a few days after at the same restaurant with a different girl. After the meal he went straight to a certain very important officer at the War Office.

"I want to ask you something, sir," he said.

"Ask away."

"Do we contemplate any action against the Belgian Coast—it is necessary that I should know?"

"If you mean do we intend landing troops there—the answer is no," said the officer. "Later there may be naval action designed to stop up the submarine bolts but it is rather a remote contingency."

"Do the Germans believe we intend action?"

The officer nodded.

"They have strengthened the coast defences enormously," he said. "The beach is wired and mined and all preparations taken."

"Do they know we know of these measures?"

"Surely. There are daily air reconnaissances—photographic and otherwise. You can't hide these things, and in fact we have put in a great deal of counter-battery work. Indeed, our action has rather encouraged their belief that we intend opening an attack here. They have ten divisions in reserve behind that bit of coast. So long as we can keep them immobilized we shall be content."

"Would those ten divisions count heavily in another part of the field?"

"Good heavens yes! In the present condition of the German's reserves—they haven't been able to release any men from the eastern front, though it looks as if the Russian is finished for the year. It would be superfluous to tell you that what I say is vitally secret—even the Cabinet neither asks nor expects to know our plans in this respect."

Haynes nodded slowly.

"What would the information be worth to the enemy—definitely I mean?"

The staff man laughed.

"A lot," he said briefly.

"One question more, would it be worth while, from the German's point of view, to take a tremendous amount of trouble and to spend, say, half a million dollars to secure this information?"

"Five millions," replied the other, "and it would be cheap."

Major Haynes took two hours off. He wanted to think things out—and particularly his luncheon with a red-haired girl who had been unusually nervous. Not an ordinary type of chorus girl either, though she was indubitably dancing at the Hippoleum. So nervous, that twice she had opened her little handbag in quest of a handkerchief and then had been content to look vacantly into its interior.

"What a pretty bag," Haynes had said taking it from her—and then clumsily dropping it on the floor.

Before he had picked it up (with many apologies) from beneath the table where it had fallen, he had opened the bag and extracted the folded paper which she had been consulting.

That half sheet of paper covered with neat writing was the subject of his cogitations for exactly two hours. Stretched on a couch in his severely-furnished study he patiently created a working hypothesis. His reverie was interrupted as he hoped it would be by the arrival of a stocky, clean-shaven man who was ushered, hat in hand, into the room.

"Hullo Barton—any luck?"

The man seated himself and produced a notebook before he replied.

"Got all you want to know sir," he said. "The red-haired dame you left outside of the 'Café Lisa' took a taxi (No. 74171) to the Piccadilly Palace Hotel—room engaged yesterday and occupied since. She told the clerk she was expecting a 'phone call which was to be put through to her room."

Haynes nodded.

"From a call office of course—well?"

"I saw the manager, gave him my card and waited in the 'phone exchange until the call came. Here is the conversation."

"Man or woman?"

"Man sir—evidently an agent. Shall I read my notes, they're short?"

"Go ahead."

The detective opened his book and read.

Man: Did you see him?

Girl: Yes—I've just left him.

Man: Did you speak about Ostend?

Girl: Yes: See here, are you sure that that tale you told me about his being secretly married to a Belgian girl in Ostend is true? Did he really desert her?

Man: Of course. Did he tell you anything?

Girl: He said it was going to be attacked but he didn't seem worried about his wife.

Man: Did he say when?

Girl: This month.

Man: Did he seem suspicious?

Girl: No—why should he be?

Man: Did you ask all the questions written down on the paper?

Girl: Yes.

Man: Have you burnt the paper?

Girl: Yes.

("Such prevarication! as Heine would say," murmured Haynes)

Man: Did he say that he had been asked about Ostend before?

Girl: No."

"That was the end of the conversation," said the detective closing his book.

"And a good end, Barton—secretly married I think you said—so all this talk of Ostend is to arouse in me the remorseful thoughts of my deserted wife. Thank you, Barton—send a translation of your notes to the office."

He lay thinking for another half hour and then he went back to his office, and Dane, looking up from the mass of papers which invariably engulfed him, noted (with disapproval, for Dane was a serious youth) that the eye of his superior was gay, his step was light and—this he could have discovered without raising his eyes from his work—the tune he whistled was exceedingly flat.

Haynes sat at his unlittered desk, jerked open a drawer noisily (Dane shuddered), produced a pad of scribbling paper and wrote as he extemporized unmusically.

"A dismal old devil called Dane
Had a cabinet-file for a brain—"

"Do you mind sir?" said the patient young man. "I hate interfering with your harmony, but Colonel Carsland has given me rather a delicate job to do—the précis of the evidence in the Bothmann trial has fallen into enemy hands."

Haynes stopped singing.

"The devil it has—who told you?"

"The general. The F.O. Intelligence have reported the matter and there is considerable trouble."

Haynes was serious now.

"That's the fourth précis they've had this year—what are you doing?"

"Checking the précis with the evidence—the F.O. has sent us a translation of the document which has been published In the Vossische Zeitung."

Haynes put down his pen and walked across to his subordinate.

"When you've finished and have written your report, let me have it—you ought to be finished by seven."

"It will be finished in half an hour sir," said Dane.

"It will be finished at seven," repeated Haynes firmly, "in two hours and a half."

"But the colonel wants to see it before he goes home," protested Dane.

"I myself with my own hands will take it to him," said Haynes, "but I will see it first."

"But—"

"Quit butting and say 'Yes sir'," said Haynes threateningly, "and don't sigh—great Moses, Dane, who would believe that you are the fellow who burgled the Kriegsministerium in the year 1913—you are developing too lawfully, my lad."

"But will you tell me sir, what am I to tell the colonel?" demanded the exasperated Dane.

"Tell him that one of the most important documents is in my private safe and that I am out."

"But you're not out," wailed Dane.

"Good-bye," said Haynes and made a rapid exit.

In obedience to telephonic instructions Dane waited on his chief at seven o'clock, the rendezvous being Haynes' chambers.

"Here's the report," he said with quiet resignation, "I've had an awful time with the colonel. He is bringing the matter to the attention of the general tomorrow."

Haynes took the report and slipped it in his pocket.

"Blow the colonel," he said, "come and have dinner—I want you to meet one of the most wonderful heads of hair—"

"Thanks," said Dane hastily, "I've a dinner engagement elsewhere."

At nine o'clock that night, when a fuming Assistant-Director, drinking coffee in the bosom of his family, was discussing the undiscipline of people who had not had the advantage of a military training, Major Haynes was announced.

"Show him into the study—no, let him come here," said the colonel. "You can stay, Miss Withers, and you my dear," to his stately wife, "you wanted to see this fellow—I hope you won't be disappointed— ah, good evening, Major, this is an unexpected honour."

Haynes beamed. Sarcasm light or heavy was wasted upon him.

"I've brought the report colonel—so sorry I delayed it."

"My wife..." introduced the colonel gruffly, "Miss Withers," he indicated the third party whom Haynes guessed was the governess—that "charming young lady living a sheltered life"—who had been interested by his curious passion for red hair.

"We've heard so much about you," said Mrs. Carsland, waving him to a chair, "such terrible stories, Major!"

"My dear," murmured the colonel mildly.

He was less of a fire-eater in his own family circle, Haynes noted with amusement.

"Oh, I'm sure there's nothing wrong in it," smiled the lady. "Miss Withers is awfully interested—aren't you," she turned to the girl. "You see, she has—er—auburn hair!" she laughed.

The girl laughed too and Haynes laughed.

"That's why I'm going to arrest her," he said. "Rosa—you wouldn't like your little hand shattered by a pistol bullet, would you? But that's what will happen to you if your hand doesn't come out of that pocket empty. Good girl."

He leant over and caught her by the arm, dropped his hand to the panel pocket in her skirt and deftly removed the small Browning pistol she carried.

"Rosa was clever," explained Haynes when he made his report to his chief, "but she made one mistake."

"Did you know that she was Carsland's governess?"

"I suspected. But her papers were in absolute order. She even had her birth certificate and had planted her references. For three months the Red-Haired idea caught. She was in doubt whether I was looking for her and suspected her presence in England, or whether my weakness was a real one. With true German thoroughness she exploited my passion and at the same time kept herself out of harm's way.

The chorus girls were coached and well paid—new jewellery, furs and clothes were the perquisites. They were told that their employer was a friend of my deserted wife and that the mention of Ostend would certainly arouse the most poignant emotions in my bosom. Rosa used to write out the questions which were to be asked—unfortunately she used Colonel Carsland's stationery one day and that was enough to convict her."

The general looked grave.

"You think that the missing précis was also extracted through the colonel—he used to work on them at home I remember?"

"I wouldn't be too hard on the colonel," said Haynes, "these red-haired girls are really awfully fascinating."

Edgar Wallace – A Short Biography

Richard Horatio Edgar Wallace was born on the 1st April 1875 at 7 Ashburnham Grove, Greenwich. His mother, Mary Jane "Polly" Richards was born into an Irish Catholic family in Liverpool in 1843 and had worked in theatres, both as an actress in bit-parts and as a stagehand and usherette, until she married a Merchant Navy Captain, Joseph Richards, in 1867. He too had been born into an Irish Catholic family in Liverpool. His father had also been a Captain in the Merchant Navy, and his mother's family had a marine background. Mary was eight months pregnant with Joseph's child when he died at sea, and it was once the child had been born that she first turned to the stage, taking the stage name Polly Richards.

She joined the Marriott family theatre troupe in 1872. It was managed by Mrs. Alice Edgar, Richard Edgar, Grace Edgar, Adeline Edgar and Richard Horatio Edgar, Wallace's father. In late 1874 Mary and Richard Horatio Edgar had a brief sexual encounter at the party following a successful show, and she fell pregnant. Worried about the scandal which would ensue and fearing that she might forever lose her job at the troupe, she fabricated an obligation in Greenwich would detain her there for at least six months. She lived in a room in the boarding house on Ashburnham Grove until her son, Edgar, was born. She had already made preparations through her midwife for a couple to foster the child, and when Edgar was born the midwife presented her with Mrs Freeman. Her husband was a fishmonger at Billingsgate market and she already had ten children. She was happy to foster the child and for Polly to make frequent visits to see him in exchange for a small sum of money which Polly made from her work in the theatre troupe.

Wallace was now known as Richard Horatio Edgar Freeman, taking his father's forenames and his foster family's surname. Broadly speaking his childhood was a happy one. The Freemans looked after him lovingly and he had good friendships with his foster siblings, particularly Clara Freeman, twenty years his senior, who often looked after him as a child. After a few years Polly's finances tightened and she was no longer in a position to afford the fee she had been paying the Freemans. However, they had grown to love the young Wallace and opted to adopt him in order to keep him out of the workhouse. Polly could no longer visit him. George Freeman was keen to ensure that he had equal opportunities and did all he could to secure him an education at St. Alfege with St. Peter's, a Peckham boarding school. Despite his adoptive father's efforts, though, Wallace left the school aged twelve for truancy.

Instead he went to work and by the time he was fourteen or fifteen he had experience selling newspapers at Ludgate Circus, near Fleet Street, as a worker in a rubber factory, as a shoe shop assistant, as a milk delivery boy and as a ship's cook. He stole from the milk company which resulted in his dismissal, and in 1894 was engaged to a local girl from Deptford named Edith Anstree, though he broke this off and instead joined the Infantry. He adopted the name Edgar Wallace which he took from Lew Wallace, the author of *Ben-Hur*, and his medical record records a diminutive 33" chest and a stunted growth. his first posting was with the West Kent Regiment in South Africa in 1896, though he did not enjoy military life, arranging to be transferred to the Royal Army Medical Corps. Though this was a less strenuous job, it was also significantly less pleasant and so he again transferred to the Press Corps, which he found suited him far better.

He was in Cape Town in 1898 where he met Rudyard Kipling and was inspired to begin writing and publishing poetry and songs. His first collection of ballads, *The Mission that Failed!* and was enough of a success that in 1899 he paid his way out of the armed forces in order to turn to writing full time. His first work was as a war correspondent for Reuters who kept him in Africa to cover the Boer War, and then for the Daily Mail in 1900 and various other periodicals after that. It was while he was in South Africa that he met and married Ivy Maude Caldecott, who was 21 when they married in 1901, despite her Wesleyan missionary father's strong opposition to the union, for several reasons, one of which was that Wallace's writing was not turning quite the profit he had expected it would. *War and Other Poems* and *Writ in Barracks,* both published in 1900, had not proved as popular as his first collection. Eleanor Clare Hellier Wallace, their first child, died of meningitis in 1903 and, in rather deep debt, they returned to London. Wallace used his contacts with the Daily Mail to get work with them in London, electing to write detective novels as a means of making quick money.

Wallace met Polly, his birth mother, in 1903. He didn't remember her from his childhood as he had been too young when she became unable to visit, so it was as though they were meeting for the first time. She was sixty years old and terminally ill, living in abject poverty. She had come to Wallace seeking financial support, but he turned her away. She died in the Bradford Infirmary later that year. In 1904 he and Ivy had a son, Bryan. He was still writing and had completed his first thriller, *The Four Just Men*. Since nobody would publish it he resorted to setting up his own publishing company which he called Tallis Press and he published a serialised version of *The Four Just Men* in 1905. He received promotional assistance from the Daily Mail in which he ran a competition for entrants to guess the method of murder in the final chapter, with a prize of £1,000 for a correct guess. Although the paper's proprietor, Lord Alfred Harmsworth, refused Wallace the £1,000 prize money, Wallace persisted and went ahead with the competition, recklessly advertising on billboards and buses all over the country, hoping to expand his advertisements across the Empire. His worried colleagues at the Daily Mail managed to convince him to lower the prize money to £500, split into a first prize of £250, a second prize of £200 and a third of £50, but with the total cost of his advertisements nearing £2,000 he would need to sell £2,500 worth of copies before he could see any profit. He was confident that this could be achieved in just three months.

Though he had remarkable enthusiasm, it became clear that his managerial skills left a lot to be desired. It soon emerged that nowhere in the competition terms and conditions had he included a clause limiting the competition to one single winner; instead, any entrant with a winning answer was entitled to their corresponding prize money. Thus, if ten entrants guessed the first prize answer, the competition was obliged to pay each entrant £250. This error was only noticed after the competition had been closed and the solution had been printed in the final installment of the novel, meaning that not only was there no opportunity to write his way out of enormous financial obligation, but the entrants who had guessed correctly would by now have read the final chapter and know they had done so. £250 was an enormous amount of money to the average Edwardian family and those entitled to it were likely to make a lot of noise if they didn't receive their money. Despite this, Wallace's fist instinct was to attempt to ignore the issue entirely, even as he discovered that he initial calculations had been dramatically over-enthusiastic and it would take nearer to two years of continuous sales to break even at the initial cost of £2,500, let alone the new figure which included every correct guesser. Compounding the problem even further was the awful realisation that as sales continued throughout the initial three month period and Wallace approached the £2,500 break-even figure, new readers were still eligible to enter and guess correctly. Though it is unknown how much he eventually owed his readers, Lord Harmsworth found himself having to loan over £5,000 in order to protect the reputation of the newspaper, since 1906 had come around and there still hadn't been a list printed of all prize-winners. It was less a charitable act than one of a man anxious that the failure would reflect ill on his own paper. Wallace filed for bankruptcy shortly thereafter and as a token gesture to his creditors sold the rights to the novel to Sir George Newnes, a publisher and editor, for £75. In the midst of this chaos though, Wallace managed to write and published *Smithy*, which would become the first of a series of *Smithy* novels.

Following this fiascos Wallace was dismissed from the Daily Mail in 1907 when inaccuracies which were found in his reporting, resulting in libel cases being brought against the paper. That year he became the first reporter to be fired from the Daily Mail and was his awful reputation prevented him from finding work at any other papers. Despite all this, though, he travelled to the Congo Free State later that year and reported on the criminal treatment of the Congolese people by King Leopold II of Belgium and the Belgian rubber companies. Up to fifteen million Congolese were killed in various atrocities, and Wallace was asked to serialise stories based on his experiences for her penny magazine *Weekly Tale-Teller*. He and Ivy had another daughter, named Patricia, in 1908. Though his new work for *Weekly Tale-Teller* was bringing in some money, their financial situation was still dire and Ivy was occasionally forced to sell off her jewellery and possessions in order to pay for food. In 1911 his Congolese stories were published in a collection called *Sanders of the River*, which quickly became a bestseller. He would publish eleven more such collections featuring a total of 102 stories of adventure and tribal life set on the river Congo.

From 1908 he started to enjoy a revival of both his success and his reputation. The majority of his initial writing he sold outright in order to make money as quickly as possible and placate his creditors in the United Kingdom and South Africa, but as his success saw the reestablishment of his reputation he began to find work once again as a journalist, beginning in horse racing for the *Week-End*, the *Evening News* and then as an editor for the *Week-End Racing Supplement*. Following this success he started his own racing papers, *Bibury's* and *R. E. Walton's Weekly*, eventually buying his own racehorses and losing thousands gambling. His success was insufficient to support his newly extravagant lifestyle and his marriage began to fail in the light of his financial irresponsibility. He and Ivy had their last child together, Michael Blair Wallace, in 1916, and she filed for divorce in 1918 moving to Tunbridge Wells with her children.

Wallace began to fall for his secretary Ethel Violet King and they married in 1921, having a child, Penelope Wallace, in 1923, who would herself go on to become a successful crime writer. Wallace now began to take his career as a fiction writer more seriously, signing with Hodder and Stoughton in 1921. He now began to organize his contracts more carefully, arranging for royalties and properly organized promotions, run by people more business-minded than himself. He was marketed as the 'King of Thrillers' and they gave him the trademark image of a trilby, a cigarette holder and a yellow Rolls Royce. He was truly prolific, capable not only of producing a 70,000 word novel in three days but of doing three novels in a row in such a manner. His publishers signed off on almost everything he wrote as soon as he turned it in, estimating that by 1928 one in four books being read at any time was written by Wallace, for alongside his famous thrillers he wrote variously in other genres, including but not limited to science fiction, non-fiction accounts of WWI which amounted to ten volumes and screen plays. Eventually he would reach the remarkable total of 170 novels, 18 stage plays and 957 short stories.

Wallace became chairman of the Press Club which to this day holds an annual Edgar Wallace Award, rewarding 'excellence in writing'. In 1923 he broadcasted a report on the Epsom Derby horse race for the British Broadcasting Company, making him the first ever radio sports correspondent. His ex-wife Ivy had suffered from breast cancer between 1923-1924, and it eventually killed her in 1926 despite a successful operation to remove a tumour the year before. He wrote the essay "The Canker in our Midst" in 1926 which dealt, aggressively and controversially, with the problem of paedophilia in show business, describing how children were unwittingly left open to sexual abuse, and linking paedophilia with homosexuality. Its tone has been described as "intolerant, blustering, kick-the-blighters-down-the-stairs". He was appointed chairman of the British Lion Film Corporation on the back of the success of *The Ringer* and on the agreement that he give British Lion first choice on all his future work. This contract gave him an annual salary and a large amount of stock with the company, along with a stipend on all British Lion production of his work and 10% of their annual profits. This extraordinary contract gave him annual earnings by 1929 of almost £50,000, or almost £2 million in 2014.

He now became an active figure in politics, entering the 1931 general election as a Liberal contestant in Blackpool, rejecting the current government in favour of free trade. He lost the election by over 33,000 votes and went to America in late 1931, once again deeply in debt after buying the *Sunday News* which closed six months later. In America he quickly found work as a script doctor for RKO Pictures, enjoying early success with the 1932 adaptation of *The Hound of the Baskervilles*. This success, along with that of the play *The Green Pack*, established his reputation in America and he was able to see his own work adapted for film, beginning with *The Four Just Men*. His most successful theatrical work, *On The Spot*, which explores the life of Al Capone, has been described as "arguably, in construction, dialogue, action, plot and resolution, still one of the finest and purest of 20th-century melodramas". These successes led to his assignation on RKO's "gorilla picture" which would become famous as King Kong in 1933.

He worked on the first draft though he was beginning to experience severe headaches which brought about a diagnosis of diabetes. Despite taking medication to address his condition, it deteriorated in a matter of days. His wife booked him passage home but soon heard that he had entered a coma and died of his condition and double pneumonia on the 7th of February 1932 in North Maple Drive, Beverly Hills. In his honour the bell at St. Bride's church on Fleet Street tolled for the duration of the morning while the flags flew at half-mast. He was buried near his home in England at Chalklands, Bourne End, in Buckinghamshire. Once again, at the time of his death he was in severe debt, mostly to racing bookkeepers, though these debts were settled within two years thanks to the enormous royalties his estate continued to receive from his contracts. His writing has been translated into 29 languages, and is considered one of the most important bodies of Colonial writing.

Edgar Wallace – A Concise Bibliography

African Novels
Sanders of the River (1911)
The People of the River (1911)
The River of Stars (1913)

Bosambo of the River (1914)
Bones (1915)
The Keepers of the King's Peace (1917)
Lieutenant Bones (1918)
Bones in London (1921)
Sandi the Kingmaker (1922)
Bones of the River (1923)
Sanders (1926)
Again Sanders (1928)

Four Just Men (Series)
The Four Just Men (1905)
The Council of Justice (1908)
The Just Men of Cordova (1917)
The Law of the Four Just Men (US title: Again the Three Just Men) (1921)
The Three Just Men (1926)
Again the Three Just Men (US title: The Law of the Three Just Men) (1929) a.k.a. Again the Three

Mr. J. G. Reeder (Series)
Room 13 (1924)
The Mind of Mr. J. G. Reeder (US title: The Murder Book of Mr. J. G. Reeder) (1925)
Terror Keep (1927)
Red Aces (1929)
The Guv'nor and Other Short Stories (US title: Mr. Reeder Returns) (1932)

Detective Sgt. (Inspector) Elk series
The Nine Bears or The Other Man or The Cheaters (1910)
revised as Silinski - Master Criminal (1930)
The Fellowship of the Frog (1925)
The Joker or The Colossus (1926)
The Twister (1928)
The India-Rubber Men (1929)
White Face (1930)

Educated Evans (Series)
Educated Evans (1924)
More Educated Evans (1926)
Good Evans (1927)

Smithy (Series)
Smithy (1905)
Smithy Abroad (1909)
Smithy and The Hun (1915)
Nobby or Smithy's Friend Nobby (1916)

Crime Novels
Angel Esquire (1908)
The Fourth Plague or Red Hand (1913)

Grey Timothy or Pallard the Punter (1913)
The Man Who Bought London (1915)
The Melody of Death (1915)
A Debt Discharged (1916)
The Tomb of T'Sin (1916)
The Secret House (1917)
The Clue of the Twisted Candle (1918)
Down under Donovan (1918)
The Man Who Knew (1918)
The Strange Lapses of Larry Loman (1918)
The Green Rust (1919)
Kate Plus Ten (1919)
The Daffodil Mystery or The Daffodil Murder (1920)
Jack O' Judgment (1920)
The Angel of Terror or The Destroying Angel (1922)
The Crimson Circle (1922)
Mr. Justice Maxwell or Take-A-Chance Anderson (1922)
The Valley of Ghosts (1922)
Captains of Souls (1923)
The Clue of the New Pin (1923)
The Green Archer (1923)
The Missing Million (1923)
The Dark Eyes of London or The Croakers (1924)
Double Dan or Diana of Kara-Kara (US Title) (1924)
The Face in the Night or The Diamond Men or The Ragged Princess (1924)
The Sinister Man (1924)
The Three Oak Mystery (1924)
The Blue Hand or Beyond Recall (1925)
The Daughters of the Night (1925)
The Gaunt Stranger or Police Work (1925) revised as The Ringer (1926)
A King by Night (1925)
The Strange Countess (1925)
The Avenger or The Hairy Arm (1926)
The Black Abbot (1926)
The Day of Uniting (1926)
The Door with Seven Locks (1926)
The Man from Morocco or Souls In Shadows or The Black (US Title) (1926)
The Million Dollar Story (1926)
The Northing Tramp or The Tramp (1926)
Penelope of the Polyantha (1926)
The Square Emerald or The Woman (1926)
The Terrible People or The Gallows' Hand (1926)
We Shall See! or The Gaol-Breakers (US Title) (1926)
The Yellow Snake or The Black Tenth (1926)
Big Foot (1927)
The Feathered Serpent or Inspector Wade or Inspector Wade and the Feathered Serpent (1927)
Flat 2 (1927)
The Forger or The Counterfeiter (1927)

Terror Keep (1927)
The Hand of Power or The Proud Sons of Ragusa (1927)
The Man Who Was Nobody (1927)
Number Six (1927)
The Squeaker or The Sign of the Leopard or The Squealer (US Title) (1927)
The Traitor's Gate (1927)
The Double (1928)
The Flying Squad (1928)
The Gunner or Gunman's Bluff (US Title) (1928)
Four Square Jane or The Fourth Square (1929)
The Golden Hades or Stamped In Gold or The Sinister Yellow Sign (1929)
The Green Ribbon (1929)
The Calendar (1930)
The Clue of the Silver Key or The Silver Key (1930)
The Lady of Ascot (1930)
The Devil Man or Sinister Street or Silver Steel
or The Life and Death of Charles Peace (1931)
The Man at the Carlton or The Mystery of Mary Grier (1931)
The Coat of Arms or The Arranways Mystery (1931)
On the Spot: Violence and Murder in Chicago (1931)
When the Gangs Came to London or Scotland Yard's Yankee Dick
or The Gangsters Come To London (1932)
The Frightened Lady or The Case of the Frightened Lady or Criminal At Large (1933)
The Green Pack (1933)
The Man Who Changed His Name (1935)
The Mouthpiece (1935)
Smoky Cell (1935)
The Table (1936)
Sanctuary Island (1936)

Other Novels
Captain Tatham of Tatham Island or Eve's Island or The Island of Galloping Gold (1909)
The Duke in the Suburbs (1909)
Private Selby (1912)
1925 - The Story of a Fatal Peace (1915)
Those Folk of Bulboro (1918)
The Book of all Power (1921)
Flying Fifty-five (1922)
The Books of Bart (1923)
Barbara on Her Own (1926)

Poetry Collections
The Mission That Failed (1898)
War and Other Poems (1900)
Writ In Barracks (1900)

Non-Fiction
Unofficial Despatches of the Anglo-Boer War (1901)

Famous Scottish Regiments (1914)
Field Marshal Sir John French (1914)
Heroes All: Gallant Deeds of the War (1914)
The Standard History of the War – Volumes 1 – 4 (1914)
Kitchener's Army and the Territorial Forces:
The Full Story of a Great Achievement (1915)
Vol. 2-4. War of the Nations (1915)
Vol. 5-7. War of the Nations (1916)
Vol. 8-9. War of the Nations (1917)
Famous Men and Battles of the British Empire (1917)
Tam of the Scouts (1918)
The Real Shell-Man: The Story of Chetwynd of Chilwell (1919)
People or Edgar Wallace by Himself (1926)
The Trial of Patrick Herbert Mahon (1928)
My Hollywood Diary (1932)

Screenplays

King Kong (1932, first draft of original screenplay, 110 pages) While the script was not used in its entirety, much of it was retained for the final screenplay.
The Hound of the Baskervilles (1932, British film)
The Squeaker (1930, British film)
Prince Gabby (1929, British film)
Mark of the Frog (1928, American film)
The Valley of Ghosts (192

Short Story Collections

The Admirable Carfew (1914)
The Adventure of Heine (1917)
Tam O' the Scouts (1918)
The Fighting Scouts (1919)
Chick (1923)
The Black Avons (1925)
The Brigand (1927)
The Mixer (1927)
This England (1927)
The Orator (1928)
The Thief in the Night (1928)
Elegant Edward (1928)
The Lone House Mystery and Other Stories (1929)
The Governor of Chi-Foo (1929)
Again the Ringer The Ringer Returns (US Title) (1929)
The Big Four or Crooks of Society (1929)
The Black or Blackmailers I Have Foiled (1929)
The Cat-Burglar (1929)
Circumstantial Evidence (1929)
Fighting Snub Reilly (1929)
For Information Received (1929)
Forty-Eight Short Stories (1929)

Planetoid 127 and The Sweizer Pump (1929)
The Ghost of Down Hill & The Queen of Sheba's Belt (1929)
The Iron Grip (1929)
The Lady of Little Hell (1929)
The Little Green Man (1929)
The Prison-Breakers (1929)
The Reporter (1929)
Killer Kay (1930)
Mrs William Jones and Bill (1930)
Forty Eight Short Stories (George Newnes Limited ca. 1930)
The Stretelli Case and Other Mystery Stories (1930)
The Terror (1930)
The Lady Called Nita (1930)
Sergeant Sir Peter or Sergeant Dunn, C.I.D. (1932)
The Scotland Yard Book of Edgar Wallace (1932)
The Steward (1932)
Nig-Nog and other humorous stories (1934)
The Last Adventure (1934)
The Woman From the East (1934) Co-written By Robert George Curtis
The Edgar Wallace Reader of Mystery and Adventure (1943)
The Undisclosed Client (1963)

Other
King Kong, with Draycott M. Dell, (1933), 28 October 1933 Cinema Weekly

Plays
An African Millionaire (1904)
The Forest of Happy Dreams (1910)
Dolly Cutting Herself (1911)
The Manager's Dream (1914)
M'Lady (1921)
Double Dan (1926)
The Mystery of room 45 (1926)
A Perfect Gentleman (1927)
The Terror (1927)
Traitors Gate (1927)
The Lad (1928)
The Man Who Changed His Name (1928)
The Squeaker (1928)
The Calendar (1929)
Persons Unknown (1929)
The Ringer (1929)
The Mouthpiece (1930)
On the Spot (1930)
Smoky Cell (1930)
The Squeaker (1930)
To Oblige A Lady (1930)
The Case of the Frightened Lady (1931)

The Old Man (1931)
The Green Pack (1932)
The Table (1932)